SENTRIES

SENTRIES

Gary Paulsen

□

Bradbury Press New York

Bradbury Press
An Affiliate of Macmillan, Inc.
866 Third Avenue, New York, N.Y. 10022
Collier Macmillan Canada, Inc.
Manufactured in the United States of America
1 2 3 4 5 6 7 8 9 10
The text of this book is set in 11 pt. Baskerville.

Library of Congress Cataloging in Publication Data:
Paulsen, Gary, Sentries.
Summary: The common theme of nuclear disaster and
human vulnerability interweaves the lives of
four young people, an Ojibway Indian, and illegal
Mexican migrant worker, a rock musician,
and a sheep rancher's daughter with the lives
of three veterans of past wars.
I. Title.
PZ7.P2843Se 1986 [Fic] 85-26978
ISBN 0-02-770100-X

This book is dedicated to my son
JIM PAULSEN
in hope

SENTRIES

1

☐ Somewhere in Minnesota

Her grandfather was still alive, that was the problem.

Sue Oldhorn was seventeen and an Ojibway Indian just out of school and at her first job, a real job at a bank running the accounts computer, and none of that was a problem. She had money and lived at home and would soon get a new car, well, not new but new-used—a blue Mustang— and none of that was a problem.

But there was this . . . this difficulty. She worked hard all day and came home where her mother and her grandfather waited—her father had been gone many years—and it was always the same.

Always the same.

She would sit down to the meal her mother had prepared, usually with food that Sue had bought with her money from her new job, and before she could eat, before she could even began to eat her grandfather would start.

Always the same.

"You are young," he would say. "You are young and now you must listen. Now you must listen to this story."

But he was old, very old with deep wrinkles not just in his face but deep wrinkles in his mind and when she thought of it at work sometimes, sitting at the computer console with the green numbers rolling before her—when she thought of it she thought that he was still alive, and that was the problem.

He has lived beyond the time when he should have lived, she thought, but not in the hard way it sounded. Not then. He was still alive and he remembered things that did not always fit with the way he lived now, in the small house on the outside of town with two women who took care of him and fed him. He was still alive and in the wrinkles in his mind he remembered things to tell in his stories—oh, God, she thought, sitting at the computer. Such things he remembered.

He was still alive and last night when she came home to sit down to supper before the date she had with Bob from the bank, Bob who was tall and not a Robert but a Bob, Bob who smiled inside—when she came home before a date with that Bob her grandfather had put his fork down and she sighed inwardly and even openly and put her fork down as well.

"You are young," he started. "You are young and a woman but now hear this story. Hear this story. . . ."

And he had begun the story of the two arrows, which he had told many other times and which was never the same, never the same. It was a story of a time gone, so far and long gone that even the Indians were different. It was the story of when a family was starving and a man had gone hunting with only two arrows in his quiver.

He had first found a rabbit, but didn't want to use his arrows for so little meat. Then he came upon a deer, and still he wanted more, and finally a moose and he had shot one arrow at the moose but the moose had too much magic and the arrow had turned away. When he shot the second arrow it also missed, and the man had no food for his family and so he returned in shame at his greed and pride, and she knew the moral of the story. Knew it well.

But it was an old story. A boring story. And he told it in the old singsong sound she did not like, told it differently each time as if he couldn't remember it well enough to keep it straight. Sometimes two arrows, sometimes three, sometimes a rabbit, sometimes a grouse, and on and on and it bored her sideways.

He always waited until they were sitting down to eat and that always made them eat cold food because he became angry if they ate while he talked and it always seemed as if he wanted to tell the story when she was trying to hurry to get to work or about to leave on a date or just anything to make it inconvenient and she hated the stories.

Hated them.

Because they were boring but more, too. She hated them because at final look they weren't true. He was old and told the stories and she didn't believe them and didn't want to believe them because they had nothing to do with her life. Nothing to do with the bank or the new-used Mustang or the date with Bob who smiled inside or the fact that it was her check that bought the food that was now getting cold while she waited. Waited.

Her grandfather was still alive, and she sat now with her fingers slamming against the keys on the computer harder and harder, her forehead tightening into a frown, anger coming through. She was of a time and age that he could or would never understand because he didn't see things as they were now but as they had been. Her grandfather was still alive.

That was the problem.

2

☐ Somewhere in New Mexico

He was fourteen and he had come across the river in the night blackness, in the desert dark he had come across, alone. That's how he made the picture in his mind as he stood in the darkness alone on the U.S. side of the river. He had done it.

"I am fourteen and I am in the United States and things will become right now. I will find work and there will be money to send home and there will be food for them."

His name was David Garcia and he was thin with a slight curve to his back and a bush of black hair that needed to be cut. He had the high, strong cheekbones and straight lines of his dead father, killed in a fight of honor, and his eyes were a quiet, serious gray. His arms were corded and tough, as were his legs, and he wore a tired-looking cap with CAT across the front and he carried a worn old army knapsack as old as the Second World War. In the knapsack were a pair of socks, two oranges he had taken from a stand in Juárez when the wind was right for taking them, and nothing else. Nothing.

He had come up from Chihuahua by stealing a ride on the train, had crossed the boundary river at night without the aid of coyotes—those who helped people cross for money and sometimes stole from them or, worse, killed them—and he felt pride that he had done it alone.

He was making his way north, far north, because it was early summer and all the work was in the north now. Men who came back told of the work in the northern states in the early summer. There were sugar beets to thin with the hoe, and the farmers paid much money for the work and would hire anybody who was willing to do it.

"For every hour you are paid three dollars," the men said in the cantina when they drank the warm beer and talked. "That is how it works out. For every hour you are paid three dollars American and there is food, *frijoles* with some meat for one meal a day, and a place to sleep. A dry place to sleep. And you don't have to be too careful about the authorities in those northern states. There are not many and they do not leave their offices in the big cities."

David had listened to them many times. He cleaned the cantina in the mornings before it opened; the early drinkers were working men who came into the cool, dark, and private place to sip a warm *cerveza* before they went out into the heat of the day. Many of them had gone north to work and come back, or been deported back to Mexico, and they talked constantly of when they would go again and where they would go and where they would find work when they did go. Day after day they talked of the money they would make when they went north, money to send back for their families, and David listened.

He lived with his mother and five brothers and sisters on the outskirts of Chihuahua in an adobe hut with a metal roof. They were not poor because—in David's mind—they had never had enough to be even poor. There must be something to compare to, he thought. To be poor you must have at one time had something. Anything. They had nothing. Food for one day had to be worked for that day. Every day. And they had meat once a month, if that. Usually it was rice and beans and some peppers.

There was work for him. There was much work for him in Mexico. But there was nothing to be paid for the work and so he listened to the men talk, listened to their stories and remembered them, and one day when the wind was right for going, he had told his mother he was heading north.

"As they all do," she had answered, nodding. "That is to be expected."

"I will send money," he told her. "And when I come back I will bring money. I will bring it all."

This time she had said nothing but dug in a sack she had by the mat on which she slept and handed him the pair of socks. He had gone that night, gone on the train north to Juárez to hide during the day and slide across the muddy river at night.

There had not been a moon, which helped, but there had been many others crossing and the border patrol had been busy with their trucks and helicopters running searchlights back and forth and he had barely missed capture at least three times.

Once across the river he had walked north all night until he stood now, just before dawn, on the edge of a highway that stretched into the northern darkness like a line pulling him. It was a slow time for traffic but they had talked of this, too, the men in the cantina, and he knew that he could hitchhike and somebody would give him a ride sooner or later. Then he had only to keep going until he got to the beet fields in South Dakota, keep catching rides, and he could then work. He knew that.

A car came and he heard the slick-wet whine of the tires on the asphalt before he saw the lights come over the slight rise to his rear. He stood sideways and held out his thumb but the car did not stop.

Four more cars came and went and did not stop but the fifth driver pulled over, and when David got to the car he found it to be a young man in a suit who said he was a salesman and was going to Denver. He spoke Spanish roughly to David but enough was understandable. Way up to Denver, David thought when he said it, and he climbed in and wished he could speak English but said thank you, thank you, and leaned back in the soft seat as the car gathered speed.

He was truly heading north now. Denver was almost to South Dakota and the beet fields.

☐ Somewhere in Montana

Laura Hayes left the house and headed for the barn with long strides. It was close to eight and the school bus would be coming down the highway soon. But if she hurried she just had time to talk to her father. She was a tall girl and when she covered ground it was with an effortless purpose that seemed to make her float. She wore jeans and a jeans jacket and had long hair but kept it up for convenience. She didn't really think much about her appearance as long as she was comfortable.

At the barn she took a quick look inside, down the dusty open middle. She saw nobody and went around the side and back to the rear where she came up to an old man leaning on the fence gazing across a large pen with just over seven hundred pregnant ewes in it.

"Hi, Louie—where's Dad?"

Louie hesitated and studied the sheep before turning. He was very old, perhaps eighty, though Laura wasn't sure, and stiff and sore with old bones so that he moved slowly. "Soon, now. Tonight. Early tonight they will be starting to get sick. They be sick later tonight."

Laura smiled. He meant that they would start having lambs but he was so old-fashioned that he thought it wrong to talk of such things in front of young girls, even seniors in high school, as Laura was; so he said they were getting "sick," when he really meant they would be going into labor. Which in turn meant that the hardest time of work on their small ranch was about to begin. Lambing meant up to two weeks with virtually no sleep, moving sheep with their lambs into the holding pens until they got to know the lambs well enough not to lose them in a herd, doctoring ewes that had problems—it was an endless time, a tearing hard time and Laura loved it; she loved it as she loved all of ranching. "I was kind of looking for Dad," she repeated. Louie was starting to forget things, she knew, and he needed to be nudged now and then. He was the best man with sheep in the world, which was why her father kept the old Basque on the place and made him part of the family, but he had to be nudged now and then. "I need to talk to him."

"Ahh, your father, he be in town. He say he be back in two, mebbe three hours." Louie said "fadder" for father and "tree" for three but she understood him in spite of the accent. Sometimes she caught herself saying things the same way. Especially after working with Louie a long time, like during lambing. "He go for more medicine and more shells for the flat rifle because the coyotes they be coming in when they smell the ewes getting sick."

Laura nodded. He would have gone for antibiotics for the sheep. Any time a ewe looked sideways at you, it was best to give it a shot. They died so easy, so easy—any help was worth trying. And the "flat rifle" was what Louie called the .243 they used for shooting coyotes. He called it that because it was so fast it seemed to shoot flat and never drop. Laura hated shooting the coyotes but they were drawn in by the smell of the afterbirth and took a terrible toll on the lambs if they weren't put down. She had seen them working the lambs, pulling and tearing, and knew it had to be done; anybody who saw them working the lambs, taking them down, knew the coyotes had to be taken out. Still, she didn't like it.

Laura studied the sheep. She had started as a small girl by helping her mother in the house more than working outside. But over the years she had kept less and less to the house. She was happier outside. She liked the air, liked the open, and sometimes stayed with the sheep a week or two when they took them up into the high country for summer pasture on the leased meadowland. Louie was there, too, of course, but she worked the herd with the two collies they had—Mutt and Jeff—and she knew sheep. She knew the country and she knew how to ride and work dogs and she knew sheep. She wasn't as good as her father, and nowhere close to Louie—who was so good with them it was almost strange—but she knew sheep. She could see now that Louie was right. They were ready to start coming in, many of them. She would stay home from school.

"I'll go in and change into my work clothes," she said to Louie. "If they're going to start lambing I'll have to stay and help."

Louie shook his head without turning from the

sheep. "No. Your father he say that you go to school this time."

"What?"

"He say go to school this time this year."

"But I always stay home for lambing. Always." Laura wheeled to go to the house, then turned back. "Always!"

Louie said no more but kept looking at the sheep, his head shaking with slow little motions, and Laura knew that it would do no good to talk to him. Louie was just passing on orders from her dad.

She started for the house but out on the highway she could see the school bus coming. If she went in to talk to her mother she would miss the bus and if her father said she had to go to school, that was it. She could discuss it tonight with both of them, but she'd better not miss the bus.

Turning again, she trotted up the driveway to meet the bus. But all the way she was thinking she always stayed home for lambing. Ever since she was in first grade.

☐ Somewhere in California

He stood to the side of the party and watched for a while. It was a good party, or as good as any of them were. He had been to many of them. That was what he did. Make music and party.

His bass player, sunken-looking Jimmy, came by with a new girl on his arm. He always had a new girl on his arm. She smiled at him, locked her arm more tightly in Jimmy's, and steered him into a wide space where they could dance.

"Hi, Pete, want to do a line?"

Peter Shackleton turned and saw somebody holding out a piece of flat cardboard with the small white lines of powder on it, and he shook his head. He had been shaking his head for a long time now but nobody noticed. "No. I'm fine like I am. I'm even now. It's all right."

It's because of the band, he thought. Peter had started a band called Shackleton's Ice two years earlier, in his last year in high school. They had worked hard and done some school gigs and one thing led to another—always with hard work—and they had cut a record. There was talk now of a bullet and they had a good sound, a really good sound. It was a tight sound, controlled but right on the edge of going radically insane—one reviewer had called them "controlled madness." A new sound.

It was Peter's sound. He had worked hard to make it, worked hard to write the right kind of songs for the sound they made; he had been shaking his head to the white lines for a long time but they didn't see it. And that's the band thing, he thought. They assumed that because he was with the band and ran the band that he would like the white lines of powder.

But he didn't. When he tried it he hadn't liked it. He didn't like it now as he did not like drinking or smoking or anything else that changed his clarity, changed the way he saw or felt life.

Right now he was seeing and feeling the party

for what it really was—Hollywood. The song "Hollywood" rippled through his mind while he stood there and he looked at everyone, looked at the party and felt the current of what was happening. He tried to see the song of what was there, the beat and movement of it, but all he felt was the current.

Party current. He tried to remember why Sheldon had set the party up. Sheldon Schwartz was their agent-manager and he was good, but too busy for Peter, too busy-busy. He was always having them be at parties, having them appear at charity gigs, having them work college dances or state fairs, and after a while none of it meant anything. They were just things to do, and more things to do, until the parties mixed with the gigs and the fairs and the colleges all slid together and all that was left to Peter were the currents.

Party current. Somebody running around with a piece of cardboard covered with lines of white powder that would change your music, change the way you saw the music and songs. Loud sounds of laughter and dancing and music—always music from Shackleton's Ice—and pretty girls and pretty men and producers and mike people and Sheldon hovering around like a great bird, making certain that everything was right.

Party current. A beautiful girl with short hair and wide eyes came up to him and smiled and said how much she loved his music and he smiled in return and thanked her and she touched him on the hand, a small touch. He knew what it meant but pretended not to know and asked what she liked most about his music. Which song.

"Oh," she answered. "All of them. . . ."

Which of course meant that she didn't really know much about any of them but wanted to know Peter, and he let his smile slide down at the corners until it was vague and told her that he had to talk to his agent and moved away as politely as he could because such feelings never worked. Not what she wanted. It was the same business as the man going around with the white lines on the cardboard and it didn't work in the same way.

Party current. Mike came up to him and stood for a moment, staring at Peter's face. At first Peter thought it was something important. But in a few seconds he could tell that Mike was just stoned and Peter gave him a grin. "Having a good time?" It was a totally unnecessary question since Mike, who played keyboards and looked like Gregory Peck in *Moby Dick*, loved to party and always, always had a good time. But Peter asked anyway.

"Incredible," Mike answered. "It's just incredible."

"What is?"

Mike turned away, swiveled, let his eyes go around the room at the entire scene, then back to Peter. "This. All this. It's incredible. Two years ago we were in high school and I couldn't afford to fill my car with gas. Now we're tearing The Town apart (he always called Hollywood "The Town") and we can have anything we want. That's what's incredible. I love it. I love it."

Peter nodded. "Me, too."

But, he thought. Nothing more than that. Just but. He could feel the current, and the undercurrent, and the under-undercurrent, but. He wanted to make it and liked the idea that they had a bullet and was happy about all of his life, but.

Mike turned away and pushed through the smoke and noise of the party and left Peter standing by the door alone and he thought: But.

Just that. But.

Party current.

5

≡ Battle Hymn One

When it happened to him Timothy Johnson was nineteen years old and had been in Vietnam for seven months. It always happened to somebody else until it happened to him.

Tim was a marine rifleman. He had been on several sweep-and-destroy missions, deployed by helicopter. On two occasions he had faced the worst that can happen in helicopter deployment —he had entered "hot L-Z's," landing areas being swept by enemy fire. And he had not been hit. Men were hit around him, but he had not been hit and like many others he thought he would somehow never be hit. Somehow. Once he had come down and the helicopter he was jumping out of took several rounds in the engine and burst into flames and fell nearly on him, a large fireball, but he had scrabbled and run sideways on his hands and knees and while his clothing was burned and his pack was heated until some of the ration packages in it melted, he did not get hurt. He thought somehow he would never be hurt. They called him lucky with a capital L. Lucky. And he was, somehow. Lucky.

When he had been In-Country for four months he was sent out on ambush. It was his first exposure to enemy fire and he found it exhilarating. They had set up a trail block, he and five other men, and they were supposed to wait there until midday because the enemy had been moving supplies and somebody Up There wanted them stopped. So they had deployed their Claymore mines and set up their M-60 to cover the intersection in the dark and when false dawn came they still had no contact. But at first real light Tim, who was in a position forward and on the right side, saw a man coming down the trail— actually saw an enemy, which he found later happened rarely—and he waited, silently, as the man came into the ambush followed by six others.

When the lead enemy tripped the first Claymore the marines all opened up. Tim couldn't see how anybody could have come through it alive. He fired and fired until he thought he had used four or five clips in his M-16, just tearing them up on full automatic—what they called "rock and roll"—and the other marines did the same until the officer with them ordered them, screaming, to stop.

There was no movement, no return fire, but they found only one body: the body of the first enemy who had tripped the Claymore. The fragments from the antipersonnel mine at close range had caused massive damage; Tim had never before seen the effects of a Claymore so he had trouble with that. But not with the action.

Later that night, in the bunker-tent back in the compound, he talked to his friend A.J.

"I loved it."

"You're crazy, man. Your brain is fried. Nobody likes a firefight."

"I know it's not cool. But hell, A.J., you're my friend. I can tell you what I mean even when it's not cool. I don't care if I'm cool. I still liked it. I liked the power or something. I liked it."

"You're crazy," A.J. repeated. "Nobody can like what happens in a firefight. Nobody."

So Tim hadn't talked any more about it, though

it had been the truth. That first time he liked it. Even when he heard the rounds coming close around his head he thought it was all right, even when he heard the little snapping sounds they made, he thought it was still something to be, a marine in a firefight. The best of what there was to be.

Then, two months later, A.J. took a round and that was when Tim began to realize that he didn't like it. Tim was on a small sweep into a hamlet and A.J. was walking point and an AK had opened up and A.J. took a round through the chest, the right side of his chest, and he went down like a sack of dirt or grain, just flopped down, and they all returned fire.

This time Tim didn't like it. He knew A.J. was dead and he didn't like the firefight but he still didn't think he would ever be hit.

It always happened to somebody else.

When it came, he was nineteen years old and had been In-Country for seven months and he was walking down a path in a supposedly "safe" area and then something happened, and when he next knew anything about anything he was in a hospital in Saigon and was not all there and for almost every hour of every day when the drugs were worn off he tried to remember how he came to be there. All they knew was that he was hit. They did not know how, or by what—only that he was involved in some kind of explosion, some kind of flat-crack explosion with a dust-acrid smell in it that hung in his nostrils and would hang in his nostrils for the rest of his life.

"It's the stink of my arms and legs going," he says. "The stink of my body going. The smell of that explosion."

Violent damage that causes loss of a limb in combat, by explosion, is referred to officially as "traumatic amputation." Tim suffered "traumatic amputations" of the left leg at the knee, the right leg in midthigh, the left arm at the elbow, and the right arm at about midbicep. He also suffered massive lacerations across his torso, which left a network of welt-scars across the front of his body and partial loss of vision in his left eye. There is still a lot of iron in him. That's how he puts it.

"There's still a lot of iron in me. Too damn much. I can't get through the beepers at the airports."

Which probably isn't true but it doesn't matter because Tim rarely goes anywhere and then never by plane. He lives in a small room in a care home for disabled people and the walls of the room are

covered with posters from the seventies and pictures of Lennon and Harrison and he listens to
the Beatles and Jefferson Airplane—not Star-
ship, but Airplane—and the only time he can get
the smell in his nostrils to go away for a time is
when he smokes and listens to loud music. Which
he does often.

He is thirty-four years old and nothing in his
life has come or been the way he thought it would
come or be when he was nineteen and it was
always happening to somebody else; nothing, and
when asked if he is bitter, he answers with another
question.

"Wouldn't you be?"

6

☐ Somewhere in Minnesota

Then there was the date and it turned out all wrong. Everything was turning out wrong and Sue didn't know how to stop it.

Bob had come by at eight and said they were going to dinner and a movie and that would have been all right. He was driving a new car, a surprise, which he had just picked up that day. It was a Camaro and still had the new-car smell and he looked nice, really nice, and she liked him. She really did like him—which made the rest of the night seem even more insane.

On dates before they had had a good time, they laughed, sometimes they played what Bob called "a little slap and tickle," and it was easy for them to be with each other. Natural.

This time . . .

Bob had picked her up and they had gone to Smitty's, a pizza place that also served other good Italian food and they ordered and it was still all right. She needed to eat because she had not eaten at home. Her grandfather had ruined the meal. But before their food arrived, a young Indian man—she did not know him—came into Smitty's. He had been drinking and Bob had raised his eyebrow and she had gotten defensive.

Bob had said nothing. Meant nothing. But it was still there, the feeling—inside her; she thought it had something to do with her grandfather and when the young Indian man, who turned out to be named Alan, approached their booth and stood staring down at her she had become intensely uncomfortable.

At first, for a long time—it seemed a year— Alan made no sound but simply stood, weaving slightly with the drink, staring down at her. She didn't know why but a surge came up in her, a feeling she didn't understand, and she wanted to smile at him and tell him that it was all right. But before she could say anything Bob had stood, angrily.

"Listen," he'd said. "Whatever you're trying to do we don't want it around here. Take off."

Still Alan said nothing. Sue realized that one of her hands had come up, come up like a bird to reach out to Alan who seemed somehow hurt, but she forced it back down to the table. She could not take her eyes off Alan, however—it felt as if their eyes were locked together somehow, as if he were asking something that she was supposed to know the answer to. . . .

"Damn it, clear out of here!"

"I am not whole," Alan said, ignoring Bob completely. Then he smiled down at Sue. "Are you whole?"

She didn't know what he meant or know what any of this was supposed to mean, and she shook her head.

"I'll call the manager!"

Now Alan looked at Bob for the first time and Sue realized that the Indian man had truly not seen him before. There had been only Sue. He looked at Bob and Sue could sense the danger there, sense the controlled danger in Alan and knew that she could do nothing to stop it. But before it could grow into an explosion Alan turned back to her. "Are you whole?"

And before she could answer he turned away

and walked, slowly, weaving carefully, out of Smitty's. Bob had turned back to her and there was concern in his eyes, but something more, too, something she did not at first understand but then realized was disgust.

Because Alan was drunk, she thought.

Or because Alan was an Indian?

Or because Alan was a drunk Indian?

The question was a hot worm in her brain. Bob sat there, looking at her, and he did not appear to think of her as Indian. But what if she got drunk? Where was the line drawn—if she got drunk would he think of her the same way? And the thought brought Alan back to her mind, brought back the business of being whole, which she did not see or understand and which, strangely, made her think of her grandfather—all at Smitty's, all before dinner and a movie with Bob who was nice and whom she really, really liked.

But all through dinner and later at the movie she thought of how Alan had looked: coal-black hair and a red handkerchief headband, standing by the table, weaving with the drink, studying her. She could have been anybody, anybody, but she wasn't. She was an Indian. She could have been anybody with Alan looking down at her. . . . Once a portrait artist had stopped her in the mall and done a sketch of her and told her she looked Polynesian or like a beautiful Eurasian, and Sue had thought that fine because she did not want to look like what she thought of as a squaw. She could be anybody. Anybody.

But she wasn't.

She was an Indian.

And her grandfather was still alive and that night—the next night after her date—he told a story at the table.

"Now listen," he said. "You are young and a woman. Now listen to this story. . . ."

He told of the huge battle they had had in the long ago time, the battle with the whites who were then called the long knives because they carried swords.

It was a story she had heard many times before, since she was a small girl. It was a story with much blood and fighting and violence, a story of brave warriors in a village who had been attacked by a large force of soldiers who came thundering in on their horses, shooting and hacking with their swords, meaning to kill everything in sight.

"So now they came," he said, singing in the high-pitched voice that went up and down like water over gravel. "So now they came and we heard the small sounds from the straps and buckles on their saddles and were prepared for them, hiding from them, and we took many of them down though we had only two guns and had to use arrows. We took many of them down and we wiped those long knives out. We worked hard that day in the dust from their horses' hooves and the screams of the wounded, we worked hard and long that day and when that day was done the long knives knew never to come against us again.

"We lost many, too, but not as many as the long knives lost. When we were done they knew not to fight again. Not us. We wiped them from the earth.

"So now they came and we fought them in this way and they were no more. . . ."

He told the story, but she had gone to the library and checked and knew that such a battle never came to the Ojibway. They were Ojibway and they had never fought the whites. They had fought only the Sioux, only other Indians when they came to fight. The Sioux had fought and killed many whites in the uprisings of the 1850s but the Ojibway had not.

Her grandfather was still alive and he told the story of the great battle with the soldiers but she had even written to the library down in Minneapolis where they had all the records and found that there had never been such a battle, found that the soldiers had never ridden against the Ojibway.

Her grandfather was still alive and he told the story of the blood and the dust and she had checked and found him to be born in the 1920s, which would make him a small baby at least fifty years after any such fight could have taken place; at least fifty years after there was any blood or dust or listening to the small sounds from the saddles and straps.

Her grandfather was still alive and he told the story about the big fight with the long knives that she knew to be all lies, all lies, because she had checked when she was in high school, had called everybody and checked with everybody to make certain because she wanted it to be true. Her grandfather was still alive and told the stories that were a lie and she was sick of hearing them.

Sick of it.

And yet, and yet this time, looking down at the cold food when the story was done, it was different. It was all different this time; somehow, though he told the same story and she knew it was a lie, Sue could see some parts of it.

She could see the dust and blood and hear the screams, looking down at her cold potatoes. She could hear the small *thwuck* of the arrows hitting the soldiers and the horses, see the brown running backs of the warriors—and why could she see what was a lie this time and not have seen it before?

And why did she think of Alan when her grandfather who was still alive told the story of the fight with the long knives?

Why did she see Alan standing next to the table, staring down at her with his hurt, sad eyes?

All of that was new and it was new in a way that did not fit with what she had wanted to become; did not fit with the accounts computer at the bank or Bob who was really nice and who smiled inside and her blue almost-new Mustang and the fact that she looked like a Polynesian or Eurasian.

Her grandfather was still alive and why did she want to ask him what it meant to be whole?

7

☐ Somewhere in New Mexico

The ride to Denver took sixteen hours and David learned much about being in Estados Unidos from Art Deleon, the man driving the big car. Deleon was a salesman of some kind of office equipment or machinery. David couldn't be sure because he understood almost no English and Deleon spoke a broken Denver version of Spanish that David had trouble following.

He found that Deleon was from Denver, had been born and gone to school in Denver, but was of Mexican parents. He understood coming north to work because that is what brought his parents north many years before. Deleon had friends who helped the people who came north to work, if David wanted help, but it was probably not necessary since David was on the right path by hitchhiking up into the Dakotas to hoe beets. There were even some sugar beets to hoe around Denver but there were so many people there to work them that it would undoubtedly be better for David to go north. . . .

All this he learned in broken Spanish while the car bored north through the desert night, all night. David dozed in spots, caught little bits of sleep here and there and let Deleon's talk wash over him. He thought how lucky he was to get a ride, one ride, that took him all the way up to Colorado. He thought that when they were halfway he would eat one of his oranges because he was getting very hungry and very thirsty now, sitting in the car as it floated along the highway. But he would not know when they were halfway so he would have to ask Deleon to tell him because he did not want to eat the orange too soon. It could be long before he got food and he wanted to pace it out correctly. He did not mind going without food. Sometimes he went without food for two or three days at home. That was the way of it. But everything rolled together before he could ask and he went into a deeper sleep and did not know how long he slept this time, or would have slept, except that Deleon put a hand on his shoulder and shook him awake.

"We are in Santa Fe. We are going to stop to eat. What would you like?"

David looked out the window, rubbed the sleep out of his eyes, and saw they were at a hamburger place with a speaker for ordering. "I am not hungry." It was, of course, a lie. He was starving. But he had no money and he would not ask for help.

"I understand," Deleon said, smiling. "My parents came that way—like I told you. I understand. I think it would be all right for me to buy you some food, wouldn't it?"

David looked out the window. "I will have money, when I work, I could get it to you if you give me your address."

Deleon nodded, dropping the smile, becoming serious. "That would be fine. That would be acceptable."

Deleon ordered breakfast, muffins and sausage and eggs and some fried potatoes with coffee and some hot chocolate. Double everything—great piles of food that came in sacks steaming hot with the smell of cooked meat and eggs and potatoes —and he handed most of it over to David as they drove out. "Go ahead and start. I have to keep driving so we'll eat as we go."

David reached into the sack and brought out containers and opened them and began eating. He was so hungry his jaws ached when he chewed, little dull pains at the rear, coming forward, but he chewed slowly, let the taste go all through his body. He ate until he was full and there was still much food left.

"I can't eat more," he said. "My stomach has become small."

"It will keep. Put it in a sack and save it for when I drop you off."

From Santa Fe they drove north up into the high deserts by Taos, then across the mountains at Loveta Pass and into the prairie. David had seen places on television at the cantina, places with water and oceans and fields of green, and sometimes at the cinema when the luck was right and he could get in the back door he saw movies of tropics. But he was of the desert, the sand desert, the hot desert, and to go through pines and running water and to see the snow still on the peaks—he had never seen snow—and come down the long run out of Loveta and see the prairie stretched out to the horizon took him completely.

"So much," he mumbled, looking out the window. "There is so much . . ."

"What? I didn't hear you."

"Nothing. It's just so big. One never thinks of it being big. When they talked in the cantina of coming north to work it was as if you were there and then you were with the beets. It was not clear that you had to cross so much country. It is big."

Deleon smiled. "Yes. Wait till you see the crops up north. It's as green as a pool table and just as flat."

They ran the highway up along the front of the Rockies through Pueblo and Colorado Springs and finally into the outskirts of Denver. Smog hung yellow and thick in the late-afternoon sun, but the downtown buildings stood above the yellow and David thought it was the biggest thing he had ever seen.

"Denver." Deleon pointed with his chin. "I live over that way, to the left, but I will take you to the other side of the city or you might have trouble. They check for green cards here, the police. You don't want to be checked."

"I owe you much," David said. "Thank you."

"For nothing. I told you, my parents came that way."

When he had driven the freeways through

Denver and out the north side of the city, to where the highway was back in the country, Deleon pulled over. He held out his hand. "You stay on this highway and keep going north. When you get into South Dakota there are many sugar-beet fields. Just stop at the first one where you see people working and they will give you a hoe. Good luck."

When David opened his hand there was a ten-dollar bill in it and he tried to give it back but Deleon insisted, kept pushing it at David and so he finally kept it. But he had Deleon's address and he vowed to repay the money. And when he finally got his pack out of the backseat and the sack of food from the hamburger stand and watched Deleon drive back toward Denver, he felt as if he had lost an old friend.

But see, he thought, looking in his hand. See now what I have and I had nothing earlier this day. I have money now, and food, and I am close to where I wish to go.

There is much luck to this, he thought, shouldering the pack and starting to walk, waiting for the next car. There is much luck to this and all my luck is good.

All my luck is good.

☐ Somewhere in Montana

Laura ate quickly. It was a lambing-time supper, a big pot of stew on the stove and you took a bowl and a spoon and slab of bread when you could. There would be no formal sit-down meals until lambing was finished, and then it would be hectic until they got the herd up to the summer pasture with Louie.

Her mother was helping in the barn with the lambing and Laura hurried the food to get out and help. She ate the stew half-cold, sitting alone at the table, chewing carefully and thinking while she ate. Something new was happening, something she didn't understand, and she figured to get to the bottom of it. Yet she knew she had to be careful.

Her father was what Laura thought of as a one-way kind of person, hard outside sometimes but usually fair. Almost always fair. But when he said a thing, that's the way it was and the way it stayed and Laura would have to be cautious about changing anything. And she meant to make a change. She was being cut out of things, or felt she was, and she meant to change that.

When she finished she went to the sink and rinsed the bowl and spoon with hot water and put them in the dish rack and then headed up to her room. It took her seconds to shuck out of her school clothes and throw on her work jeans and rough boots. It was cooling off outside and would be a long night, so she put on a sweatshirt with a wool shirt over that and a stocking cap. Back down on the rear porch she found work gloves and stuck them in her pocket.

She stopped on the back steps and studied the western sky with an experienced eye. Some clouds were building there and all their weather came from the west and it could mean rain. Or worse, sometimes it brought snow, sometimes wild blizzards could hit when they went into lambing and that would kill sheep. Everything killed sheep.

This time it looked like rain, though, and while that wasn't good it was better than snow. Large clouds curved over the mountains to the west, bringing evening a little earlier than it would normally come, and Laura let the cool wind from the front take away the feeling of school. It was always a change when she came home, as if school were a dream world and this was the only real place: the storms, the sheep, the mountains. All of that was real. School seemed not to fit with how she really lived. Today had been all tests, and none of them seemed to fit her life. Friday math tests didn't work with coyotes tearing lambs down. . . .

Just inside the barn door she had to stop to let the smell work in. It was the same every year. The lambing smell, the smell of ammonia from the sheep urine built up in the barn, was like a wall when you stepped in the door. It caught at the back of your throat, hung there, and you had to let it down slowly to hold the air. Strong, thick, it was at first unpleasant but it was the smell of life, of lambs, and it was as much a part of sheep ranching as the hot-wet smell of afterbirth or the lanolin in the wool.

The barn had been broken down into the forty lambing pens, twenty small pens down each side, with a slightly larger gathering pen at the back, just in front of the door, with a ten-foot-wide aisle down the middle. When she had left for school in the morning the barn was open, empty, and dusty.

Now it was full. Full of noise, thick rich smell, moving wool backs, her mother and father working the sheep, lights already on to be ready for the night. They were at the other end of the barn and waved at her when she came in. She waved back and started toward them but her mother yelled.

"Get the hair spray—we have a downer."

Laura nodded and went back to the tack room. They kept a can of cheap hair spray there for fooling the ewes. Each year during lambing a certain percentage of the ewes died, also a certain percentage of the lambs. But ewes and lambs didn't often die together so it was necessary to get some surviving ewes to take lambs from the dead mothers. The ewes would not do this naturally, and in the old days the shepherds used to skin out the dead lamb and put the skin over the new lamb. All ewes recognized the smell of their own lamb and the skin would often fool them.

But so would cheap hair spray. It was a simple matter to spray the back of the lamb, then squirt a little shot into the ewe's nostrils. Then they just put the lamb under her nose and after that she would let the new lamb nurse without any trouble. Laura smiled, thinking: the spray smells so strong we could probably get them to adopt a chicken if we sprayed it on thick enough.

"It was a young ewe," her mother said. "Too young to be a downer. It doesn't make sense."

Laura nodded but said nothing. Her mother didn't say die or death, ever—always called them downers when they died. It had something to do with her mother's father and when he passed away, but Laura had never asked about it. Apparently her grandfather had died at home when Laura's mother was alone with him and it had shocked her or hurt her deeply.

"How many?" Laura asked her father. "How many so far?"

Her father shrugged. "Not certain. One hundred fifty to one sixty. Louie's cutting the stick outside as he brings them in."

"How many downers?"

Another shrug. "Seven ewes. Nine lambs. You want to take the front pens?"

"Sure."

Her mother sprayed the back of the lamb and squirted some in the new ewe's nose and pushed-pulled the ewe to the standing pens in the rear as Laura moved to the front of the barn—the end toward the pastures and the holding pens outside.

The procedure was simple, if tiring. Out in the back there was a large pen with the pregnant ewes—less a pen than a small pasture, really. Louie watched this pen, watched the ewes, with Mutt and Jeff, the two collies. When a ewe started to go into labor, went down in the birthing curve and began pushing, Louie watched her. If there was trouble he would drag-carry her to the barn and put her inside at once. Or if the ewe died he brought the lamb or lambs in. Most of them threw twins. If the lambs died he brought the ewe into the barn.

As soon as the lambs were born, outside, he took a piece of gunnysack and wiped the afterbirth off the tight new wool and carried the lambs into the barn. The ewe would get up and follow, worried, making the small worried sounds they make to talk to the lambs. Inside the barn the ewe was put in a holding pen, alone, with her lambs, so she could get used to them and used to the smell of them and know them before being placed in a second pen with more sheep—ten or twelve ewes—where she could get accustomed to having her lambs with other lambs. Finally she was placed back outside in a different pen-pasture with more ewes and their lambs. If this procedure were not followed it was quite possible for the ewe to become confused and not know her own lambs in the crowd. It had to be gradual, had to be slow, and it made for a lot of hard work. When the Hayeses were working seven hundred ewes that threw mostly twins the total came up close to two thousand animals, ewes and lambs both, they had to process and watch and care for—"plenty work," Louie said about lambing. "Plenty good work."

Outside, as Louie brought each sheep in, he cut a notch in a stick by the door. Ten notches were separated with a space, then ten more—slow, careful cutting with his old pocketknife. Laura asked her father once why Louie didn't just take a pencil and notebook and keep track and her father hadn't answered at first but looked out in the pen where Louie was working the dogs. "They always notched in the old days. My daddy used to notch and his daddy notched. It's part of sheep, the notching. That's why he does it."

Mutt and Jeff helped Louie. They circled at the back of the herd, back and forth, and held them in tight so Louie didn't have to chase all over the place for the ewes when they "got sick."

Moving back there the dogs also helped to keep the coyotes away. They didn't come during the day, but sometimes at night, even with the lights under the peak of the barn, the coyotes would come in, working the shadows like gray sharks, popping ewes or lambs if they were born before Louie could get to them. Once her father had shot across the herd to kill a coyote on the other side and had shot low and taken the back out of a ewe. He got the coyote but it killed the ewe as well and her mother bit her lower lip and went to the house and her father never shot low across the herd after that.

But the dogs helped. They didn't go after the coyotes but just their being there kept the coyotes away, or mostly, and Laura couldn't watch them without being amazed, after all the years with dogs. They were friendly animals, and would come to her and be petted, or to her father or mother. They could be fed by anyone. They loved children. But if Louie were anywhere around they were his. No, more than that, they were him. They watched his hands and eyes and many times did things he wanted them to do before he actually gave an order. They had been with Louie for seven years, when he got two pups out of the same litter, and they were worth ten men on horses when it came to working sheep, and they were as much a part of Louie as his arms.

Laura stopped by the front pens and studied the ewes. They all looked good, were up, with the new lambs nursing, butting with their heads to make the milk flow, hitting so hard sometimes they almost lifted the ewe off the ground.

She went to the sliding door and looked out the narrow opening they had made to put ewes and lambs through. Louie was standing by the door, smoking his pipe, watching the herd. In the evening light his face looked almost like metal, as if cast, the smoke dribbling out between his lips as he puffed on the old black stem. When he heard her he turned and smiled around the pipe.

"You are home. That is good."

"Yes. It is. How they looking?"

"Good. Good so far." He nodded. "But there is weather coming in. Mebbe snow. We will be working hard for a few days if the weather isn't good to us." He said "wedder" for "weather."

"Lots of work," Laura agreed. "But there always is—come lambing."

But Louie had gone to see about a sick ewe. Laura watched him go, his old back bent in the thick folds of the ancient corduroy jacket he wore, the smoke coming from his pipe back around his head as he walked through the sheep to get to the sick one.

Lots of work, she thought, and when will I get to talk to Dad about what's happening around here?

☐ Somewhere in California

"All right, all right, this is it, by God. This is it. This is it."

Sheldon had a way of raising his voice and saying things twice when he got excited and he was fairly exploding now. Peter and Mike were sitting in his office getting the rundown on the next gig. The rest of the band was scattered around town, recovering from the party. Peter never had to recover because he didn't get involved in parties that way and Mike never recovered because he said the shock to his system would be too much.

"You know what I've got for you? You know what I've got for you?"

Peter smiled. Mike was sitting with his eyes closed and he could either have been sleeping or meditating or going into a coma. Sheldon was always excited, though usually not to this level. Still, he was an agent and agents had a way of making everything sound better than it was; Peter had gone through a different agent before Sheldon, a flat rip-off agent named Perme. The whole experience had been a disaster, but he had learned a lot. He had learned that agents tend to make things sound better than they really are.

"What have you got for us?" Peter let his long legs stretch out on the floor ahead of the chair and slouched down. Sheldon's secretary, Joannie, came in with coffee and he took a cup gratefully. "What's so wonderful?"

"You won't believe it—you won't even believe it."

"Try us." Mike spoke without opening his eyes. "Don't keep us in suspense."

Peter grinned openly. He had known Mike for four years, since they had been in school; Mike had a way of cutting through the jungle.

"I talked to Moses in Colorado. We've got a gig for you at Red Rocks." Sheldon laid it on the line. "Red Rocks, right? You know what that means?"

"It means we have to go to Colorado," Mike

said, with his eyes still closed. "We've never played Colorado. We won't know who to party with. Doing Red Rocks means we'll have to bring our own party. That's what it means."

"It means you've made it." Sheldon kept his voice patient. "A lot of groups would kill to make Red Rocks."

It was true. Peter knew it was true and for a second or two he felt excited. But the feeling from the party was still on him. The undercurrent. It wasn't a down feeling, wasn't negative so much as a kind of waiting.

A kind of waiting.

He stood. Red Rocks was where everybody wanted to perform. It was an outside gig and pulled everybody in Denver and Denver was a good town for performing. They would make a lot of money, Shackleton's Ice, but more than that it would kick their album up and they would, truly, have made it. They could get a plane, instead of chartering all the time, and from Red Rocks they would only do bigger and better concerts, more records that sold more copies, more money until they . . . what? Until they peaked. "That's good, Sheldon. Really good."

Sheldon leaned back in his chair and looked at them. "So what's the matter? I give you the world and you act like I laid a disease on you. What's happening here?"

Mike shrugged. "My head is still where I left it last night. No big thing."

"Yeah," Peter agreed. "Same here—heavy party."

With that he turned and left. He wasn't sure until he got to the door just what he was going to do or where he was going, but he felt like moving. When he got outside he realized that he wanted to go work on a new song, more than a song, a new sound that had been kicking around in his head.

It was the sound that went with waiting. A kind of sound that went with a kind of waiting.

"Wait a minute." Mike caught up with him in the parking lot. It was hot already and the smog made them both squint—the smog and the early-afternoon sun. "Where you going?"

Peter shrugged. "Home. Got some work to do."

"You all right?" Mike opened his 'Vette door to let the hot air out. He was parked next to Peter's Trans-Am. "You're acting kind of side-ways lately."

"What do you mean?"

"I mean you never party and there's something bugging you. Want to talk about it?"

They were friends, partners in a way, but they seldom talked about personal problems or feelings beyond the band. Besides, Peter didn't know for sure what was bothering him, or even if anything was, just that he felt a new sound coming on. "I just want to work. Not perform, but get it down, you know?"

"You got something new coming?"

Peter nodded. "I think so."

"And it feels good?"

"I think so."

"That's it, then." Mike got into his car and slammed the door. "I'll leave you alone. Write if you get work."

He tore out of the parking lot by Sheldon's agency's building and Peter got into his car and turned on the air conditioner.

He would work. Maybe he could get the new sound down. If he got home to his keyboard and guitar maybe he could get it down in time for the Red Rocks gig. He pulled out into traffic and let the car drive itself down Melrose Avenue toward Malibu, steering automatically. His mind started doing what he called rolling, passing images and ideas through his thoughts like the flopping picture of a poorly adjusted television screen. When this happened it was as if he had no control but could stop it when he wanted to lock it down and think about a single idea.

Got to call my folks, he thought. He hadn't spoken to his parents in two weeks and they lived just fourteen blocks from his beach cottage in Malibu. They thought he had become a drugged-out rocker, he knew—they were certain of it. When he tried to tell his father once that he didn't use, didn't like what it did to his sound, that he had (he smiled, thinking of this) an "investment portfolio" at a brokerage house and couldn't have been more "normal" except that he had a good sound, his father just shook his head. All he saw were the smoky nights, the gigs, the parties.

Sad, too, Peter thought. He kind of liked his father and mother. It was too bad they didn't understand. Another smile. My parents don't understand me. Even that was "normal." I am a music maker and my parents don't understand me, don't want to understand me. Poor me. Or is it that I don't understand my parents? Poor them.

A street girl with orange-painted hair recognized him through the window of the car at a red light and came toward him. The light changed before she drew close and he went on. Usually they didn't recognize him unless he was dressed for performing. When he put on the dark turtle-neck and pants and slicked his hair back they had him. They knew him. But wearing jeans and a T-shirt and shades kept him pretty well hidden.

Roll. New thought. Too much time on parents or fans.

And Jan. Have to talk to Jan. Jan with the long legs and the wide eyes who said she had gotten sick of waiting for him to be sensible and decided to go crazy with him. And of course he wasn't crazy at all but only let people think he was for the sound. The sound. Jan who ran on the beach with her Labrador dog named Willet; Jan who had her own life but wanted to share his as well, share equally, but didn't quite understand the sound as his parents did not quite understand the sound and tried to separate the sound and Peter as if the sound were a job he could leave each day. They did not understand that when the sound was cut, Peter bled—there was not a line between Peter and the sound, not a dividing space. The sound was Peter and Peter was the sound and he was thinking of his parents again, wasn't he? No, maybe not, maybe his parents and Jan together.

Roll. New picture.

The sound. His thoughts jumped to Kansas City. They had, in the early days, played an auditorium or something there, he couldn't remember. A big building, lots of noise, not like later when they got known, but a rough night with a small crowd they weren't sure about. After it was over—and it had not been good—they had gone out to party, always to party, and he and Mike had wound up with two girls in a black bar somewhere in Kansas City and at first Peter had not felt safe. But they had live music at the bar, a tough old Kansas City blues band with older people—God, he thought, in their fifties and sixties at least—and an old piano with keys missing and dented horns but the damnedest sound, the damnedest sound he'd ever heard. It made him cry and he could see Mike crying as well. They had some guitars against the wall and a mouth harp and he and Mike started to jam with them, rough at first, but coming on, coming on, and when it finally hit and they triggered and were together he had never felt anything like it. At one point he looked over to the lady playing the piano, who was old and had no teeth and he thought was named Pearl, he looked at her and had never seen anybody or anything so wonderfully beautiful in his life. She just kept the chords going for them and they built around it and whenever there was a pause or slow-down she filled it with everything she had ever been or done, just filled every hole they left with sound, moving up and down, letting the music carry her, and when they were done for that night, when the light came into the greasy front windows of the bar at dawn and they had to leave and make their plane, Mike said, "Ahh, hell, let's stay."

"No," Pearl had said, smiling toothlessly. "You be the wrong color. You ain't bad, but you be the wrong color. You got to be shade nine to stay, like we are. But that was fine anyway, wasn't it fine?"

Roll. A cop waved at him when he went past the squad car sitting at the side and he wondered if the cop knew him or was just friendly. He hit the Pacific Coast highway and turned left. Close to home now. Get into the cottage and get to work. The sound was coming now, was on him, and he had to get it down—maybe get it done in time for Red Rocks.

He was parking in his garage when he realized he'd forgotten to ask Sheldon when they were supposed to do Red Rocks.

10

☰ Battle Hymn Two

He was twenty years old and he went from a farm
in North Dakota where he had been raising potatoes to the inside of a B-17 bomber in the skies
over Europe in 1943. He thought when it was
done he would return to raising potatoes in North
Dakota. His name was Richard Erickson.

It did not occur to him that he would not be
able to return to North Dakota to raise potatoes.
It occurred to him before he went to Europe,
during the training, that he might—only might
—be killed or injured but probably not killed, and
only injured in a remote way, what he thought
of as a flesh wound, which would heal. But it did

not occur to him that he would not be able to return to North Dakota to raise potatoes and marry the girl named Betty Nelson who said she would wait.

And did wait.

At first it was all very exciting and he hated Hitler and believed in the war and joined the air corps. He had always wanted to fly and never had and thought it might make the war "more interesting." So he joined the Army Air Corps and told them he wanted to be a pilot. They gave him many tests, most of them crazy tests, and told him something about his inner ear would keep him from being a pilot. Or a bombardier.

But he could still fly, they told him. They needed gunners, too, on the planes, and they sent him to gunnery school where he learned a great deal about the .50-caliber air-cooled machine gun, more than he ever thought he would know about any gun, and spent a lot of time shooting at towed targets.

He did well. He learned the right way to use the lead rings on the machine-gun sight and learned to identify targets correctly and could tear the target sleeves to pieces when they came by being towed by a small plane. He could even hit the target towed by when he was in a truck moving the opposite way with the machine gun mounted on a post in the back. He could hammer the rounds out and watch the tracers flow in a line, every fifth one, just holding down the little thumb-button and letting the machine gun pound against the mount as he worked the sight.

He was proud of his gunnery skills and turned out to be in the top ten in his class—actually number three—and they promoted him to private first class and told him he would be corporal before he knew it.

Corporal Richard Erickson.

He thought it had a nice ring to it and he wrote home to Betty Nelson and told her that El Paso was hot and dusty and Fort Bliss was hot and dusty but that he was doing well and would make corporal soon, which would mean a little more money to send home. He was sending money home because it would help later, after the war, when he was done and came home to plant and grow potatoes in North Dakota and marry Betty Nelson.

When he was done with gunnery school they assigned him to the Eighth Air Force and he found that he was to be sent to England. He thought that was exciting and wrote home that he would be a corporal in England and there were lots of pretty English girls, ha, ha, but that Betty didn't have to worry.

They let him fly to England. The Eighth Air Force was already over there, but he worried that he would have to take a troopship because he was afraid of water. He did not know how to swim and if the ship was torpedoed he didn't think he would have a chance. Besides, he probably would get seasick and puke his guts out on the way over, ha, ha, he wrote to Betty Nelson.

But they let him fly in a transport and he marveled at the speed of his movement. One day he was at Fort Dix, in New Jersey, and the next day he was in England and a two-and-a-half-ton truck picked him up and took him to the airstrip where his bomber was stationed.

He still had not been in a bomber. He had fired from a converted transport and knew of flying to some degree but he did not know yet what it was like in a B-17.

He found that it was not like standing in a converted transport airplane and shooting at targets on the ground as you flew by.

He found that the B-17 was a four-engine machine designed specifically for the carrying of bombs to drop on German cities and that it had ten crew members of which he was one and that they were far from invulnerable but were terribly, terribly easy to shoot down. He also found that the other crew members did not like him at first because he was "green" and as such represented a danger because he would not know what to do when the German fighters came at them.

Not *if*. But *when* the German fighters came at them.

He found that he was to be a waist gunner on the right side of the airplane, handling a machine gun that stuck out an open "window," and that he would wear a heavy sheepskin pair of pants and jacket and helmet but that there would be no other protection for him.

He found that the man he was replacing had been killed by an antiaircraft burst that had driven shrapnel through the plane and through the sheepskin suit he had been wearing. The holes were patched in the side of the airplane, the shrapnel holes that had killed the man he was replacing, but he could still see them readily— jagged tears in the aluminum skin. He thought that there must have been jagged tears in the man's flying suit and jagged tears in the body of the man who had stood there with the machine gun when the antiaircraft shell burst, but he said nothing.

Not then.

While it sobered him and made him write less lightly to Betty Nelson who would wait, Richard still did not think of the jagged tears in terms of his own body. He thought vaguely that lightning would not strike twice in the same place. And on the first two or three training flights, easy flights over England so he could learn the position and the way the gun moved, he made a point of looking out the opening and not seeing the holes in the side of the airplane.

Then came the first mission and the beginning of the hot fire of fear in his brain, what they called fear but what he knew to be worse than fear, knew to be worse than any kind of fear "they" could ever speak about. His squadron had been called up to bomb some rail junctions and he sat in the briefing and tried to take notes but was too excited. They talked of bomb loads and altitudes for the pilots, and expected fighter opposition for the gunners, and he listened but could only think of getting into the plane and getting into the sky.

But the crew was different from how they had been on the training flights. They were quiet, subdued, had even quit swearing, and they moaned when they saw the target map with the red line across it stretching into France, and did not take notes but smoked constantly and went slowly to the jeep that took them to the plane.

The mission had gone smoothly enough. They had taken off and it was all business, each position checking in as they gained altitude and met the rest of the squadron coming from other air bases. Then they had flown across the Channel and that was when Richard noticed that the other gunner had changed. His name was Ralph and he normally talked quietly, but at least talked; now he was silent, nervously chewing gum, checking and rechecking his gun and looking out the opening —then more checking the gun, more chewing, swinging the barrel of the gun back and forth. He test-fired a few rounds when called upon to do so, as did Richard, then went back to being quick and nervous and the feeling leaped across space to Richard. A spark. And at the peak of that nervousness he heard it for the first time— the warning.

"Bogies. Two o'clock! Two o'clock! Damn it, waist, let's hear some guns going!"

It was from the pilot and he was talking to Richard, the right waist gunner, who should have seen the enemy fighters on his side, up high, and didn't, couldn't see them. Finally, by squinting, he saw the specks of four fighters, tiny specks way up above him. They looked harmless, almost like spots of dirt on his goggles. Even as he watched, the lead fighter flipped over on his back and started down, followed by the other three, and Richard swung his gun to be ready to fire. But as the fighters were coming back toward the bombers there was between them a closing velocity of something near five hundred miles an hour and the specks grew rapidly into fighters, ME-109 fighters, with winking noses from the cannon fire . . . and then they were gone, gone sliding below before Richard could fire, before he could do anything.

But they had done something. The fighters had done something.

Just below Richard's plane another B-17 took the full fire from all four fighters and disintegrated in the air, started to fall apart and then exploded as its bomb load went. And where there had been ten men and a plane there was nothing but a greasy cloud and Richard knew fear, knew the metallic taste of it in his mouth, knew the feel of it, knew what they called the hot fire of it. If the German in the fighter had just raised his nose a little, if all the fighters had just pulled up their noses a bit in their dives they would have hit Richard's plane. Just a little, he thought. They just had to raise their fire a whisker and he would be gone and he knew fear, knew all about fear.

He could die.

He could be injured. Terribly.

He had the metal taste in his mouth, chewed gum quickly, nervously, swept the sky with his gun barrel, felt the tightening in his stomach that came with the metallic taste and did not think of Betty Nelson who would wait but thought only of living one minute at a time. He had all that in his mind, the fear and wanting to live, and it changed nothing.

The rest of that first mission they saw no more fighters, did not get attacked, and had good weather. Nor for the next two missions did Richard's plane come under attack. He started to think about making his prescribed number of missions and getting home. Maybe. After twenty-five missions they were sent home. Maybe. He had only to make twenty-two more missions and he could go home.

And the fourth mission started much as the others had done. They were to bomb a staging area. It was not far and they did not think there would be much fighter opposition. The people who did not have to go joked about the run. None of the pilots or bombardiers or gunners joked. Richard did not joke.

Take-off and crossing the Channel had gone well. No fighters. Richard moved his gun and chewed gum and leaned forward to see out the opening as well as he could and looked for specks high and low and everywhere in between and when he saw them, out to the side and slightly ahead, when he saw them his whole body tightened with the fear.

"Bogies," he called in over his mike. "Three o'clock."

They hung there for fifteen or twenty seconds —an eternity—about fifteen hundred yards out, studying the bomber formation. Then they pulled slightly ahead and rolled left to come in on a side pass and Richard pressed his thumb-button and started putting the stream out at the slipping fighters, pounding the rounds out to stop them, to stop them and kill them before they killed him. But the blinking noses grew larger and larger and then the whole part of the plane he was standing in was torn to pieces.

Cannon shells took it all apart, took him down, killed Ralph, blew the guns to pieces, and through it all he could see the winking noses and hear the scream of the slipstream in the holes made by the cannons. . . .

Always the scream of the wind through the holes was with him after that, and he doubled over and could not move and then could not think and then could not know anything there was to know until later. Much later.

He was hit dozens of times by cannon fragments and metal blown from the plane by the explosions of the cannon shells. Many, most, of the wounds were superficial—what he had thought of as flesh wounds. But one, one fragment had gone in his right side and transversed across his back and severed his spinal column—and from that day on he had no function from the waist down and was paralyzed and would live in a wheelchair.

He went back to North Dakota after all the therapy and healing was done and Betty Nelson was still there and would have married him, would have married Richard and said she still loved him, but Richard would not marry her. He could not grow potatoes or run a farm and he would never be able to grow potatoes and run a farm and he would not marry Betty Nelson.

"It would not have been fair," he says now. He is good in his chair but is getting older and has diabetes and his legs have atrophied and are small and he suspects that a sore on his knee that won't heal might be gangrenous. But he is good in his chair and has strong arms still and it is hard to keep up with him when walking next to him down the sidewalk. "I couldn't be a man to her, you know. Like that. It wouldn't have been fair to her to marry her. So I didn't. I never married. I never seemed to do much of anything after that."

11

☐ Somewhere in Minnesota

Oh, no, she thought. He's here. He's in the bank.
Sue cringed and tried to get lower in her seat in
back of the accounts computer. He's here looking
for me. He came to see me.

Alan had come through the glass bank doors
and stood just inside looking around. He was
wearing the same jeans jacket and red headband
he had been wearing two nights before at Smitty's
but he looked cleaner, stronger, more clear-eyed.
He swept the front and rear of the bank twice,
let his eyes slide across Sue, then walked up to
one of the teller's cages and presented a check to
be cashed.

Sue breathed easier and went back to work. She called up the next account, began to put in the figures on the checks. It was natural for him to come to the bank. It was the biggest bank in town and he probably came in a lot to do business. He hadn't been looking for her after all.

"Hello."

He stood in front of her computer terminal. In the glass cubicle to the right she saw Bob staring out at her. She looked away from him and up at Alan. "Hello."

He was silent for a time and she thought he was not going to say anything more. He took a deep breath. "I acted poorly the other night. I came to apologize for my behavior. I will take you to lunch."

No, she thought. You won't. But she didn't say it and she wondered why. "You don't have to apologize. I understand."

"What time do they release you for lunch?"

"Actually, I already have other plans. . . ."

"Please."

And there it is, she thought—either it's a yes or it's a no. But he talked so strangely, right on the edge of music, in an odd way, and she was interested by him and there was this, this thing between them that she did not understand. And,

and, and . . . "I get off at noon and have to be back at one."

"I will come at noon."

And he was gone and she went back to her computer and didn't look into the glass cubicle that housed Bob who smiled, didn't look there the rest of the morning, and at ten to twelve she rang him on the interoffice phone and told him she had other plans come up for lunch. Had to see her mother. But she knew Bob knew it was a lie.

She went out of the bank at two minutes to twelve and surprisingly Alan showed at dead-up noon by the clock on the time and temperature sign. He was walking and she met him across the street from the bank but of course Bob would have looked out and seen it all. Well, she thought, that was all right, too.

"I do not have a car," he said. "We could walk to the drugstore. I am told they make good sand-wiches."

"That's fine." Courtly, she thought. He speaks courtly. No, it's something else. His words seem to flow. "They do make good sandwiches, and they usually have a pot of soup going."

It was two blocks from the bank to the drug-store where there was a small cafe in the back and they walked the entire way in silence. Sue didn't talk because all she could think of to say were questions and they all sounded like prying —where, why, how kinds of questions.

Alan just didn't talk.

But he walked slowly for her and took her arm across the streets and when they got to the drugstore he let her go through the door first, made a point of it, and all that was surprising to her.

They took a booth back in the corner where she slid in and he sat across from her. She ordered a BLT and he took nothing but a glass of water. Then he sat silently while she ate, or took two bites. She put her sandwich down, took a sip of Coke. "Are you all right?"

He nodded. "Fine."

"You're not eating."

"This food is not correct for me."

"Not correct?"

"I only eat beans and squash, wild rice, game, and fish. Traditional foods. I will eat later when I get back to . . . when I get home."

"I see." Still, she did not pick up the sandwich. It felt strange to eat with somebody looking at her.

"Please eat," he said.

"I'm not really hungry."

"That's not true."

She thought a moment. "No. It's not. I'm starved." And what's the difference if I eat in front of him? If he doesn't want to eat that's his problem. She picked up the sandwich and took a large bite, chewed carefully, swallowed. Then a sip of Coke, another bite, chewed and swallowed. With the edge gone she leaned back in the booth and studied him.

"I am Alan," he said, answering her unasked question. "Alan Deerfoot. I am from the Leech Lake band many years ago but I have been away and just returned. I am not married. I live alone in the woods in a place on the side of a lake seven miles out of town to the north."

"You hitchhiked into town to take me to lunch?"

"No," he said. "I walked. It is not too far. Do you like the sandwich?"

"Yes. It's very good." She picked it up and took another bite. It was almost gone. She looked at her watch and found to her shock that it was also nearly one. The hour had gone by so fast—so fast. "I have to get back pretty soon."

"I understand. What time do you get off work?"

"Five o'clock. But I have to go home for dinner."

"I could wait in town until after you have eaten.

76

We could walk or go to a film." He said *film*, not *movie*. "Or go out."

And drink, she thought. "No. Not tonight. Thank you for the lunch but I have other things to do tonight."

"I understand. Tomorrow I will walk in again. Could we talk some tomorrow evening?"

And there it is again, she thought. Either it's a yes or it's a no. And part of her wanted to say yes and part of her wanted to say no and she looked at him and smiled and did not know why she smiled. "I live on the outside edge of town at One Twenty-one La Brea. I will be done eating tomorrow at seven. If you would like to come."

"I will be there."

"I have a car," she said. "Perhaps I should pick you up?"

"Not yet. I will walk in and see you tomorrow evening." He put a dollar down for the waitress and stood with Sue and paid the check and followed her out. Once on the sidewalk she turned toward the bank and he walked the other way and she watched him for a time, watched the way he walked and saw that he was wearing leather moccasins—strange she hadn't noticed that before—and when he turned the corner she went to the bank.

She felt uneasy about him somehow, but there were so many things she wanted to know that she didn't know. Questions.

She would ask questions the next time.

That night her mother had wild rice and chicken and when the food was on the table but before they started to eat her grandfather put his hands on the table at the sides of his plate and sat straight in the chair and put his head back until he was nearly looking toward the ceiling. He spoke in the song, the high song.

"Come now, hear this story. You are young and you are a woman but hear this story," he started, and Sue and her mother put their forks down and sat back in their chairs.

It was strange, but now Sue did not think in scorn that her grandfather was still alive. Instead she listened, wanted to listen for the first time in many, many years.

He told a story of growing to manhood, the story of when a young boy became a man in the time from long ago. It was a story of a boy leaving the lodges of his village, leaving the sides of the lake where his family lived, where there were many clams and good fishing, and leaving in a canoe of bark with nothing but his bow and quiver of willow arrows fletched with grouse feathers.

Sue heard it now, heard the small things and marveled at them, was amazed by the details.

He sang of the boy's moccasins and the bead-work that made a raven-head design, which his mother had done because he was of the raven and it would bring him luck on his journey. He sang of the boy's bow of ash wood, bow wood, and how the string-song sounded when the boy released an arrow, and how the arrow sounded as it cut through the air. He sang of all the things that went into the boy, sang of the woods as they were then, all the animals the boy met—sang of all of it.

She heard it all now.

He sang-talked that evening for half an hour while their food got cold and took the boy across the big lake she knew as Red Lake and out a river into the prairie to different Indians, different villages. Out in the canoe of bark, summer into fall into winter and back to spring the boy moved, living through the snow wind in a skin lodge with strangers, hunting buffalo and woodland elk.

She heard it all.

He sang of the death of the animals that the

boy needed to kill to live, sang of the wind and the stars and the nights and moons and seasons so that she saw and heard and smelled the boy's journey into manhood and when it was done, for the first time since she was a small girl, she did not pick up her fork and eat, did not want to break the feeling of what had happened with the old man's singing.

She heard.

And when he was finished and his head came forward and his hand picked up his fork Sue did not know any longer who she was. She felt the confusion that had frightened her before but now did not frighten her, a kind of confusion that felt on the edge of joy. When he was finished she looked across the table and said:

"Thank you, my grandfather."

Sue saw her mother's eyes go wide and felt her own astonishment and realized then—as though an arrow had come into her mind—realized that she had said it in the same manner as Alan had spoken that afternoon. She realized that she was changing but could not know why nor even how—just that something was new. Something was different.

12

☐ Somewhere in Nebraska

He had much trouble getting a ride from Denver and stood for many hours on the side of the freeway. Twice the highway police came down the road but the men in the cantina had talked much of the highway police and he watched constantly for them and he saw them in time and went under a nearby overpass. Finally, in the night, a man and woman in a small bus stopped and picked him up. They could speak no Spanish and he could not speak to them in English so he rolled into a ball in the back seat and slept until they let him out in Nebraska.

It was before daylight, still the middle of the

night, but warm and soft and David curled into some grass in the corner of a field and slept for two or three hours. When he awakened he ate the rest of the food from the hamburger stand, combed his hair back with his fingers, and went up onto the highway again.

He was not sure where he was, couldn't really even guess. The man in the car had told him to go to Nebraska and turn north to reach South Dakota. The couple in the bus had been smoking and had offered him some but when he tried to find out the best way to head north they only laughed and kept smoking.

They had told him he was in Nebraska and he was along some kind of river with trees but that was about all he could know. He walked beside the highway when no cars stopped for him, watching carefully for the police, and had gone perhaps a mile when he looked across the road and there were some people working in a field.

They were hoeing at plants and he guessed they were beets so he walked across the road and out into the field. When he got close he saw they were either Mexican or Mexican-American workers and he approached the oldest man in the group.

"Buenas días," he said, smiling. "I see you are hoeing the beets."

The man looked up but didn't answer. He was in the rhythm, a hoe in each hand, working down two rows, his back bent and the hoes swinging, swinging as he chopped the beets.

"Is there work for others here, hoeing the beets?" David followed alongside the working man. "My name is David. David Garcia. Could I find work here hoeing the beets?"

There were four others in the field and they worked as if he weren't even there. Three of them were women, one an older woman who was very large with pregnancy, and one was a young boy, perhaps nine or ten, and they all kept their heads down. Clearly, they did not want him to bother them. But just as clearly he had to start someplace and the beets there were as good as the beets in South Dakota.

"I am in need of work," he persisted, following the man. They had gone halfway down the length of the field now in the morning sun, in the mist of the morning sun, and the cool of evening was leaving as the heat cooked it away. "Will it offend you if I hoe these beets?"

"No." The man answered without raising. "You

may work here. You must go and ask the farmer in the white house down the ditch from the field and he will give you a hoe and you can thin the beets. There is plenty of work for all." He continued on down the field, working his two rows, and David watched him go. Then he turned and looked along the drainage ditch at the side of the field and he could see now there was a stand of cottonwoods about a mile down and inside them a house and large barn and smaller buildings.

He jumped rows to the side of the field and trotted toward the house. When he was close he heard dogs barking and he slowed and stopped until two pups came running out to greet him, all wiggles, then he proceeded into the yard. At first he saw nobody—it looked well kept up and somehow deserted at the same time. Then he saw a man in the doorway of the large building working on the front end of a tractor and David walked up to him. The farmer was wearing a gray shirt and jeans and a baseball cap with the name of a seed company on the front. He looked large and somehow all red, as if he'd been scrubbed, David thought, with a stiff brush.

David did not know what to say. He worried that the man would not be able to speak Spanish and he wondered how to say that he wanted to hoe the beets in English. So he stood and the man looked at him for a moment and smiled.

"You want to hoe?"

He spoke in broken Spanish but David knew what he meant. "*Sí*. Yes. I want to hoe."

"Have you ever done it before?"

"Sí. Many times I have hoed the beets," David lied.

"I see." The man stood away from the tractor and went to a corner of the building and came back with a hoe. "I will go with you at first to show you what I want anyway, all right? And we'll start with one hoe. If it works out you can go to two hoes. Come on."

He walked to his pickup and motioned for David to get in and drove back to the field. There he got out and went to a row of beets next to the ones the other people were hoeing.

"We plant too many, see? We have to plant too many beets to make certain that we get enough of them. But they are too many and need to be thinned. You must take out every other beet with the hoe. Like this." He sliced off the bushy green top of a young beet to show David what he meant. "Like this and this and this." The farmer went down the row and hit every other beet. "See? This way."

David nodded. "I understand."

The farmer handed him the hoe. "You are paid for what you do. For every acre you will be paid twenty-one dollars if you do it correctly. At midday I will bring some sandwiches out and when you get done tonight there will be a sit-down meal back by the house at an outside table. You will have to sleep in the barn because I'm out of room in the sleeping huts, but it's dry and clean on the seed pallets. Is that all right?"

David had missed some of it because of the man's broken Spanish but he caught the thread. He would get food and a place to sleep and—most important—he would be paid twenty-one dollars per acre. "How much is it?"

"How much is what?" The farmer had started for his pickup and turned.

"How much is an acre?" David looked down the field. "How will I know when an acre is done?"

"When you have hoed two rows the length of this field you will have done an acre." He slammed the door of his truck. "And your back will tell you as well. Your back will know when you've got an acre done."

David looked at the length of the field. Far down he could see the small figures of the others who were hoeing. It is so far, he thought. So far to hoe. But he bent to the hoe and started work.

He had never hoed beets but he had worked. He had worked much and for very little money and in places that were not nearly as pleasant as this field and these beets. Cleaning the toilets in the cantina after a night of the men drinking and fighting and getting sick, cleaning the toilets for only a few pesos and any change he found and a bean burrito each day was not as pleasant as this field of beets.

He hoed clumsily at first, the motion new to him. First he would take a few plants out of the left row, then a few out of the right, then a step forward, then a few left, a few right, a step. All the others were using two hoes and seemed to fly forward and he worked to improve himself. He would be paid for the work he did. He had to do more work.

When he had worked for half an hour he stopped and looked back and was dismayed to see that he had moved hardly at all. He would not finish an acre in a day at this rate and he wanted to do an acre each day and more, do an acre and more each day. He would have to do better.

He bent to the hoe again and decided he would not look up until he was at the end of the field, would not see anything but beets until he was done with the two rows.

When he had done this for an hour, an hour without looking up, his shoulders ached and his back ached and his hands were already blistering. The blisters broke and they bled in that hour and the beets in that hour came to be everything. He watched only the beets and saw the tops flip sideways with each cut, saw them slide into the dirt and the fresh green stump where the hoe had cut with the moisture glistening and then the next one, and the next one, the hoe taking the tops cleanly and evenly, the hoe floating out ahead and the hoe almost pulling him down the row and soon there was nothing but the beets.

There was the time before the beets and the time after the beets but everything now, in that hour, was measured by the beets, by the swing of the wooden handle of the hoe and the cut of the blade as it floated out ahead, alive in the heat of the morning sun, pulling him, always pulling him down the row. And he would think of Chihuahua and he would think of his mother and he would think of the hut with the metal roof and he would think of his brothers and sisters and he would think of his dead father and how they brought him home on a shutter from the bar bloodied from the knife wounds and he would think of the money he would be able to send back now, now that he was north and making money to send back, but it was all with the beets.

Everything was with the sun on his neck burning in and the ache in his back and his shoulders and the pain in his arms and the swinging, cutting-slicing hoe and the beets.

The beets.

13

☐ Somewhere in Montana

Laura thought of lambing as up, over, and down—like counting sheep when you wanted to get to sleep. Except that in the lambing time there was never any sleep. Just naps caught in corners, an hour here and there, and the endless, endless work of shuffling the sheep in, carrying the new lambs in and out, moving the sheep from pen to pen. After the first day and night it was all a dream. All in a dream.

By the end of the second day she was beyond tired. Images came through in snatches as did sleep, images that might have been real or might have been based on stories she'd heard but seemed real nonetheless. . . .

Louie standing by the door, smiling around his pipe, holding a lamb out to her like a present in the light of a cold dawn as snow started to fall. Like a present being passed from the dark outside world into the lighted world of the warm barn, a sweet-wet present in the falling snow. Not hard-storm snow but gentle snow, wet snow, and the lamb all new and wet, with flakes on its back, and Louie handing the lamb through the doorway—and the lamb was as young as Louie was old in her mind. They balanced and were so pretty she wanted to cry.

Louie had an old guitar strung with electric fence wire that was almost in tune and he would sit just inside the back door and strike chords on the wire and it was music. She knew it was crude but she still thought of it as music, and when she turned and looked down the barn she saw her mother and father dancing a slow, dreamy waltz in the aisle between the pens. Holding each other closely in the western swing fashion, they glided over the dusty straw, moving in time to the wire guitar until Louie stopped to get in a sick ewe and then her father looked as embarrassed as a young boy as he let her mother go and thanked her for the dance.

Maybe dream-pictures, she thought. But it didn't matter. It didn't matter if the wire-guitar music was real or the picture of her mother and father was real. As long as she thought they were real that was enough in the numbing tired feeling of the spring lambing.

Lambing.

Up, over, and down. . . . Grabbing a bowl of stew and on the second day when that ran out, sandwiches and milk and coffee and still more coffee. Sleeping on the sacks at the end of the barn, little naps, then up to move them again.

Lambs with no mothers, some that would die, lambs with no mothers to take them. . . . They go into the house in a box in back of the stove and have to be fed with a bottle and nipple every six hours, fed the formula mixed in the bucket and warmed on the stove. Laura could not feed the lambs in back of the stove without smiling and feeling warm, even when she was so tired she couldn't stand—they took the nipple so greedily and happily they could empty the bottle in a few minutes. And after she fed them by hand she knew they would follow her, all the lambs, whenever they saw her they would follow her as they would follow a mother. . . .

Sleep in the corner. Up, over, and down. . . . Her father taking the flat rifle to the back door and bracing it against the door jamb, taking in half a breath, holding it and squeezing, squeezing the trigger as he held the coyote in the scope and the cutting CRACK of the sound in back of the barn followed instantly by the snap of the bullet hitting the coyote; she knew without seeing that it would blow the coyote up. Then the dogs running for the barn because in their gentle souls they hated the gun, hated the death of it, and Louie would have to talk them into going back out to work the herd of ewes and they would turn their brown eyes to him, soft brown eyes to Louie, and finally go, slowly, until he ordered them gruffly and up across the backs of the sheep they would run to the outer side of the herd where they would work until her father took down the flat rifle again and squeezed the trigger and sent the flat death out across the sheep.

Lambing.

Up, over, and down and she saw her mother sitting on the sacks at the end of the barn, sitting asleep with some loose hair hanging down across her forehead and it made her look like a little girl, a little girl sleeping, and Laura went to her and sat next to her and pulled her head over to her shoulder and fixed the hair and let her sleep and she looked up to see her father watching her with a soft smile and it was the same smile he'd had when she saw them dancing together, a smile from some tender place inside him that she had never seen before.

Lambing.

And finally it was Sunday night and the lambs were still coming and she was still working, transferring ewes and lambs and at eleven her father came down the length of the barn and stopped in front of her.

"It's time you quit and got some sleep for school tomorrow. The bus will be coming before you know it."

"But, Dad . . ."

"Not too many buts, girl."

"Can we talk about this?" She was close to the edge, pushing up against his stubbornness and knew it. But she had taken a large measure of her will from him and had the same iron and in some ways even looked the same. He stood straight, even in exhaustion, and she had the same carriage. It was more than pride, and more than stubbornness—it was a natural attitude. Perhaps a knowledge of self. "I think we should talk about this."

Her father pushed his hat back on his head, held the smile down. "You do, eh?"

"Yes." She was serious, tired, but knowing what she wanted. "I do."

"Ahh, I see. Could we do it over coffee?"

Her mother came from the rear of the barn now, caught by their conversation. "What's up?"

"She wants to talk about going to school." Her father smiled, but there was an edge to his voice. "Thought we'd do it over coffee."

They poured coffee from the pot they kept in the end of the barn and left the lambs to Louie for a few minutes and stood in the doorway at the other end. It had stopped snowing and the sky was clear. It was getting cold but it would not get much below freezing and it wouldn't hurt the sheep or lambs. They're born with coats, Laura thought, looking out the door opening, and they came out warm and kept the heat. "Why can't I help with lambing?"

"You are." Her father took a sip of coffee. It was hot and he winced with the sting. "What do you think you've been doing?"

"I mean like always. Why am I being cut out

to the side this year? I belong to this family as much as anybody. . . ." She was getting angry and knew she had to tone it down or there would be a reaction. "Why is this year different?"

"We talked this over," her mother started. "We decided that we had kept you at the farm work too much and you might be missing something. We thought it would be best if you got a chance to see the other side of things."

"What things?"

"Well, just the other side, you know. All you get out here is the rough side of things, the hard side, the . . . the hard side. We thought you ought to maybe get away from that a little."

"But why? It's good enough for you two."

"Because we're your parents." Her father cut in. "And it's what parents do. Now, is there some other thing you'd like to talk about?"

He thinks it's over, Laura thought. But it's not. It's not started yet. "It's because I'm a girl."

"That's enough."

"But it is. I'm not arguing, but you think because I'm a girl I shouldn't be doing all this hard work. But that's wrong. This is what I am, I'm a sheep rancher. And being a girl has nothing to do with it. This is what I am and it isn't fair to cut me away from it this way!"

She had never spoken to him in such a manner and she wasn't quite sure what to expect. Anger, certainly, but what form it would take she couldn't know. She waited, standing straight. It was because she was tired, she knew; she wouldn't have said or done anything if she weren't so tired. But it was done now, done and out.

"That's enough," he repeated in a quiet voice. "That's more than enough. You go to the house and get some rest. Right now." And he turned and walked back into the barn.

Laura looked at her mother, who stood for a moment; then with eyes misting Laura walked through the darkness to the house.

14

☐ Somewhere in California

It was filling now.

Peter had closed himself in the beach house and not answered the phone for two days, two days of listening to Bach while his music-mind free-based and worked by itself on the new sound, two days of eating macaroni and cheese boiled from the little packets he picked up at the store and drinking Cokes with the phone ringing all the time and the macaroni and cheese mixing with the Bach and the Cokes and the sound and now, now it was starting to fill.

A note.

He had the first note, a high one that dropped

in the middle and he knew that could and would carry it all, carry everything he wanted to say, and it was starting to fill and he let it come.

He wrote in a spiral notebook and he could not write music but wrote in diagrams that he could understand, lines that went up and held, lines that came down or slid sideways, lines that meant the sound, little lines that moved and meant the sound. He wrote hard now, sat on the couch facing the Pacific with the glass doors open so he could hear the sound of the surf mixing with the Bach and the ringing phone and it filled and came faster and faster and then stopped. Did not end, but stopped with the feeling he knew that meant it could go on forever and he knew it was wonderful, a wonderful sound that was all he could be.

When the writing caught up with the sound he stopped and put the pencil down and looked out the window, saw the surf in the evening sun, the waves backlighted like a stage, and he was more tired than he had ever been, tired and lonely but not sad-lonely so much as rich-lonely. The loneliness that was supposed to be when the new sound came and he had to work alone, the filling loneliness that was so right because it fit the music.

Tired and hungry.

He brought some water to a boil and made

another pot of macaroni and cheese and opened a Coke and ate with a spoon and drank the Coke and let the food that didn't matter bring him back up from the exhaustion. When he was slightly better he went out on the balcony and looked at the water for a time, the waves piling in, slithering almost up to the pilings that held up the cottage, and he was amazed that he could not have smelled the sea or heard the surf for two days while he worked.

"Whacky," he said aloud, looking at the water. "Brain-fade . . ."

He went down on the sand and ran for a time, less than half a mile up and back, then sat on the balcony again. He was pushing it away now, the sound, holding it off as long as he could. He had written it but had not heard it yet except in his mind, in the chambers of his mind. He would have to work it on the guitar now and hear it, see if it sounded as good on the guitar as it did in his mind and he felt it would, knew it would but held it away as long as he could, pushing it back until he could not stop it. When it was pounding in him he went back into the cottage and turned off the stereo and took the phone off the hook and picked up his guitar and tuned it.

Then he closed his eyes and let it come, let it

100

just move around on the strings and build and flow and go from his mind down through his arms and into his fingers, and he filled the cottage with sound. At first he was not sure if he was hearing the sound as it was or hearing it as he wanted it to be, but after a time he knew it worked.

He knew it worked and he let it go out and come back and in the bouncing he knew it worked, could feel it working. When he had gone through the sound once he put the guitar down, leaned back and rested, everything down and gone, tired and wonderfully happy, filled, almost crying.

Then he turned on the reel-to-reel recorder and set up a mike and stood and went through it again, not making it bend to him but only following the sound where it led him, and when that was done he put the guitar down and rewound the tape and opened a Coke and listened to it.

It was a little shallow, but that was because he was working alone with the guitar. There had to be more to it but he knew that and could fill that part with his mind and he listened as if the group were there, playing, listened with the drums and keyboard and sax and the bass working in his mind, listened with Mike's harpoon coming in, and knew he had something really fine. Something real.

When the tape was done he pushed the button down on the phone and dialed Mike's number. It rang seventeen times and he was just going to hang up when a girl answered.

"Is Mike there?"

She giggled. "Sort of. Depends on what you mean. He's sleeping. So his body is here. I don't know where his mind is."

"Wake him up. Put him on. Tell him it's Peter and it's important."

He opened another Coke while he listened to her shaking Mike and the muffled grunting when he finally woke up and took the phone.

"Mike? You awake?"

"Are you crazy? It's four in the morning. How can I be awake? How can I be alive?"

"Good. Listen now. Get them together at the shed at nine o'clock this morning. Can you do that?"

"You got something?"

"No. I've got everything. Just get the Ice together and we'll work on it. Starting today. Can you do that?"

"It's good." Mike was totally awake now, sensing the excitement in Peter's voice. "You've got something and it's good, right?"

"I've got something," Peter agreed, "and I think it's good. I think it's really good."

He hung up and settled back in the chair by the phone, closed his eyes, let sleep take him. He needed a little rest now. He had something and it was good.

They didn't rehearse as other bands rehearsed and that was part of what the Ice was, too. Instead of taking a number and hacking and hacking and hacking it down until they could stand in a dark alley on their heads and play the number—instead of that, they took each number, each song as it stood by itself at that moment. And if they played a piece a hundred times, it was different each time, each time it was a surprise, completely new to all of them.

The "shed" they used for rehearsal was an old studio Peter and Mike had found and leased. It was on the edge of Hollywood and had probably been used at one time as a photographic studio for taking still pictures. But it was large enough for them, and isolated so their amps wouldn't destroy the neighborhood. Peter had it remodeled with sound tiles to kill the empty feeling and they called it the shed and had been rehearsing and working in it for over a year. Whenever they were in town.

Before he went to meet the Ice at the shed he called Sheldon's office and told the receptionist they would be working, and where, and he knew she would send down sandwiches and coffee and tea. They worked "clean," although now and then one of them might come up a little at first and have to work it off, and they worked hard and long, worked until "it" happened if it took a day and a night and a day.

When he got to the shed they were all there. They said nothing and Peter guessed that Mike had told them he had a new sound. He went inside and took a Coke out of the refrigerator to the right of the door. After a sip he took the reel of tape out of his coat pocket and threaded it through the machine on the stand. Then he fired up the system, let the amps warm a bit, and ran the tape.

As he knew, the sound was shallow. But they had worked with him long enough that he knew they could fill the sound in their minds and before the notes had worked ten seconds, before the note that fell off like an eagle coming out of the sun could even fade off, they had moved to their instruments on the stand at the end of the room and had started in.

Mike picked it up first, working the keys on the board gently, then Jimmy on the bass came in and Whitey brought the drums in, all of them just following the notes, not trying to take the lead, staying with them, and Peter picked up his guitar and went out ahead and it worked the first time.

Worked the first time.

It was impossible. Nothing worked the first time. But they all came in on it and followed Peter and when he took a pause to see what would happen they filled it and went on ahead and let him catch up, catch up with the note that came from the sky, and he knew they had something and so did they.

When he stopped at the end of the tape they all stopped naturally, stopped where it was finished, where it was complete, and he expected them to talk, to chatter as they always did when they worked on a new number. But they were silent.

"So . . ." he said, after a moment, a lifetime. "So . . ."

Still they were silent and at last Mike leaned

back from his keyboard and sighed. "Where did it come from?"

"I don't know. It just came. Something about that black woman in Kansas City, remember her? Something about her came into my head and that was it. That made the sound."

"It's incredible. It couldn't just come from you, not that. I've never heard . . . it couldn't just come from a person. It has to come from something else, something deeper."

"Unbelievable." Whitey stood. "Just unbelievable. You got any words?"

"Not yet. Well. Sort of. But not ironed out yet. I will tonight. I just wanted you guys to hear the sound of it so you could be working on it, filling it."

"That note," Jimmy said, leaning back and flicking the head of his guitar down in emphasis. "The one that starts up there and falls, just falls and carries the whole piece with it—that just came into your head that way?"

Peter nodded. "Clean. Like it was alive."

"Ahh, that's nice. That's really nice, isn't it?"

"Yes. It is. . . ."

"Let's do it again," Mike said, hunching over the keyboard. "Let's do it again and again. I've got some ideas—I mean, it's just incredible. Just an incredible sound."

He started it with the keyboard this time and they all followed him. And next time they would start with the bass and perhaps even the drums and Peter smiled because he knew when they got done with it the sound would have become them.

15

☰ Battle Hymn Three

They told him everything in training.

His name was Raymond Haus and they called him Ray and they told him everything he needed to know in training. Or so they said.

What he knew at first was that Harry S Truman was president and he got a letter from Harry S Truman telling him to report for induction in the U.S. Army. He knew that at first. And he knew from being told that Korea was not a war but something called a police action and he was drafted for the police action, and trained for it. Drafted and taken from his home in Pittsburgh, Pennsylvania, when he was twenty-one years old and sent to Fort Carson, Colorado, for training as a basic infantry rifleman.

He was told that his training was the finest that could be given to a soldier and that his rifle was the finest weapon ever made and was his best friend. He could not say it was wrong because he did not know any other rifles and had never held any other kind of rifle than the M1, .30 cal., gas-operated, air-cooled semiautomatic rifle he was issued and he did not have any friends.

Ray was easygoing and had been told in school that he was slow—that's how a teacher put it. "You're slow, Ray." And because he was slow and easygoing he was teased and because he was teased he didn't have any friends and so maybe they were right in training to say that his rifle was his best friend. Maybe it was his only friend.

They teased him some in the army when he first started his training. He was big, and still slow and easygoing, and so they teased him until he swatted one of them, swatted one as he'd swat a fly that was bothering him—not in anger but in annoyance—and the man had sailed across three bunks and broken his elbow on a foot locker. They had stopped teasing Ray then, but they still did not become friendly with him.

But even without friends the training went on

and he wasn't sure it was the best but he found it to be hard. Very hard. They ran him four miles every morning before breakfast and he had to do pullups and pushups every time he did something wrong, and sometimes even when he didn't do anything wrong, and that was hard because he had trouble doing things right.

They called him names, the sergeants and corporals, many names he did not like. They trained him harder and harder while they called him names and when he did not go fast enough they kicked him, sometimes hard, but he never hurt any of them except for the man he swatted and he felt bad about that. For two nights he didn't sleep thinking about swatting the man.

But when it came to working the rifle on the range he was good. He was the best. The sergeant said he was the best man with a rifle that he'd ever seen. They shot at targets from one hundred out to a thousand yards and he always hit the bull's-eye. He was so steady and sure that he always hit the black because the rifle was like a part of him and when he pointed it the bullet would go where he looked.

He was so good that they brought many men from the other units and he showed them how he could shoot. They gave him a medal that said he was an expert rifleman and told him they would give him more money each month, and he was proud and glad that they were starting to like him now.

When his first training was finished they sent him to another part of the camp and he had to learn about machine guns and mortars and bazookas and flame throwers and they did not yell at him as much and he was good with all of the weapons, so that it wasn't so bad as the first part of training and while it was hard it was not as hard. They did not make him run, which was difficult for him because he was so big, and when he could shoot all the weapons as well or better than the instructors they became still nicer to him and called him other names that were nicer.

He was sad when training was completed. But they told him it was all only part of his work in the army and that now he had to be assigned to a unit as a replacement. They put him on a plane and flew him for two days and set him off in Japan and he could not believe the things he saw for the first time. Japan was all colors and light and people yelling and more and more people still in pressing jams in the city and he thought of what he would tell them when he got home, tell them of the different people he had seen before they put him on another plane and sent him to Korea.

And it was winter in Korea, harder winter than he ever knew in Pittsburgh, but they gave him shoe pacs and a long coat and a rifle and pack and put him in a truck and sent him on bumpy roads for what seemed days and days, sleeping in the back of the truck with other men who were young and who spoke roughly and swore at him when he moved. They ate food out of small cans, as they had in training, and most of them talked of what was coming—what they called a big offensive, which he did not understand—and finally they came to a place in the middle of nothing and stopped the truck and the men were broken up into small groups and assigned to units and the bad part of the army started for him. The bad part started for Ray then because he understood that he was to fight and kill men and he did not truly believe that during training. They had said it but he did not truly believe that was what he was supposed to do, but that night he was put in a hole in the ground with a man named Stuart and in the middle of the night he heard bugles and some mortar flares went up and he could see them.

Figures in quilted uniforms were running across

the dirty snow toward him, firing small sub-machine guns in ripping bursts, and Stuart started firing his rifle in even shots, placing the bullets carefully, telling Ray to do the same.

But Ray could not shoot. He could not at first shoot at the running figures because they were men and he did not like to shoot at men, just as he did not like to swat the man for teasing him.

Stuart screamed at him again and again and Ray still would not shoot and would never have shot except that one of the small figures got close to their hole and swung his submachine gun in an arc and tore the earth next to Ray and Ray brought his rifle up and shot the man, twice, in the center of the quilted jacket.

The man went down with his legs kicking.

Then Ray knew that because he was where he was he had to shoot them or they would shoot him, the running little men in the quilted coats and pants, the small figures. And he began to fire at them and when one would fall and begin kicking he would fire on another and when that one would fall and kick he would do another, and another, and another, and he and Stuart kept up the firing until he could see no more figures to shoot at. Then the flare went out and he was glad they did not put up another flare because he sat in the corner of the hole and cried quietly, knowing that even in this way, even when he had to save his own life, it was wrong to shoot men so that they fell kicking.

Wrong.

All of what he had been told was wrong, and the next morning when the light came he went to the officer and told him that it was wrong and he could not do it any longer.

But they would not listen. The officer told him that he had to or he would go to prison and lose his right to live in the United States as a free man and many other things that frightened him. He went back to the hole with Stuart and that night the small figures came again and he shot them.

And it was not so hard that night because he saw some men the small figures killed and Ray had seen those men eating earlier in the mess line and when he saw them broken and dead with their bodies torn he felt anger at the little men in the quilted coats and so didn't mind the work so much then. He knew it was wrong, still felt that it was bad and wrong, but something told him he could not help it because the officer told him it had to be done.

And on the third night when they attacked he was ready and fired faster and killed more; but this night they sent many more men against the holes. They sent wave after wave with the noise of the bugles blaring in the dark or white-light of the flares, with the ripping tears from the submachine guns and the smoky *whap* of the grenades, and although he killed many of them, there were too many more and he and Stuart were overrun. The small figures in the light of the artillery flares ran through them and past them and hit the kitchen in the rear, then the aid station, and then came back and stopped above each hole and fired their submachine guns down into each hole. But before they could get to Ray's hole Stuart grabbed him by the collar and pulled him out.

"Run," Stuart screamed above the sound of the firing. "Run to the rear. Run now!"

He aimed Ray in the direction of the rear and they started running, throwing their rifles down, running for their lives. The flares burned out and there were no new ones and the darkness saved them. They ran in the blind darkness, ran away from the firing, ran on and on, back as far as they could run and then Stuart was hit. Ray heard the bullet hit him and Stuart went down but he was not dead and Ray picked him up and carried him over his shoulder and ran and ran.

He ran out of darkness into day, running and resting with Stuart over his shoulder, ran until he could not run any longer and his lungs were on fire and when dawn came he hid in a ditch. There was a clay culvert and he dragged Stuart in by his jacket and they lay in there all day, listening to the little men moving over and by them, and when it was dark again Ray took Stuart out and carried him until they came to a railroad track.

He did not know where he was, or where to go, and Stuart was unconscious across his back and couldn't help—so Ray simply stopped.

They did not tell him of this in training. They always said he would have a place to go, a direction to go, but he knew nothing now so he stopped and hid in some brush and cried and wished he could think better or wished that Stuart would talk or that help would come because there was too much for him and he could not understand. He worked hard to remember a good time and he remembered when he first arrived in Japan and all the colors and happy people and that made him feel better.

At the end of the third day a train came and he pulled Stuart deeper into the brush. The train stopped and there were red crosses on the side

116

of the boxcars and he saw American soldiers get out of the cars. He yelled at them and dragged Stuart out and they took him on the train. Some of them had candy and some of them had cans of food and gave him water and he ate and drank but he could not talk. He could not think. He had killed and killed and run and run and there was nothing for him anymore. He could not think.

The train started and moved slowly, filled with wounded from the battle and guarded by military policemen who were taking the wounded back to a city he could not name or think about, and he was content to sit and drink and eat the candy and be going back. He knew nothing, felt nothing. And when the train was in a cut between two small hills they ran into a barricade of torn rails and had to stop.

As soon as the train stopped they came under artillery fire. Explosions hit off to the side and men started running and screaming and taking the wounded off. At first the dirty bursts of the explosions were well wide of the train, tearing the hillside to pieces in geysers of frozen dirt and rock.

Men worked feverishly to clear the track and Korean workers were brought from a rear car to work on putting down new rails. Still the artillery exploded away from the train, but now the bursts

started to come closer, and still closer, and fragments started to hit the men working on the track.
The artillery had at first been nondirected, fired
by map coordinates, but with it coming closer it
was clear that the enemy had somehow gotten an
observer to direct the fire. After frantic searching
the men on the train saw the small figure of a
child on a hill well over a thousand yards away.
When the child raised his hands the artillery raised;
when he lowered them the artillery lowered.

There was still a lot of work to do on the rail
block and it was obviously necessary, critical, to
remove the child and so many of the men fired
at him. But he was too far and they could not hit
him and then one of the men remembered that
Ray had been an extraordinary shot in training
and they gave him the best rifle and told him to
shoot the child.

"I can't," he said. And he meant that he could
not. He could not shoot the child because he simply could not bring himself to shoot a child. It
was not the same as the quilted men who shot
down into the holes. It was not the same. But they
worked on him and talked to him, pushing the
words into his brain again and again and all the
while the artillery came closer and began to kill
men and he could see the connection between the

child and the explosions causing the screams of the wounded and he could see that no other man could hit the observer and he took the rifle and raised it and propped it on the corner of the rail car and fired and the figure spun and fell.

The small body whirled with the impact of the bullet and fell like a broken toy and he knew the child could not have been six years old, could not have started school and would not start school and would never be anything now but the broken toy on the top of the hill, and they put another child up.

Another child to raise his arms and lower his arms with the explosions and now Ray knew they would do it again and again. But he also knew that if he did not keep shooting, all the men on the train, all the wounded men and the Korean workers would be killed, and so there were two things that could not be. Two things that were impossible. He could not let them direct the artillery and he could not shoot the small bodies again and again—but if he did not shoot them everybody would die and so the rifle cracked again and another small body doubled and fell.

And again.

And again.

And again.

And twice more they put a child up and Ray fired and the child fell but it did not matter any longer, did not matter at all because the person firing the rifle was not Ray and would never be Ray again. The person firing the rifle would never be a person again. Ray's brain died with the death of the small children, died as if his brain were on the hill with the children, and indeed when that terrible time was done and Ray's prowess with a rifle had kept them from being blown to pieces and the train was moving again he turned the rifle on himself, put the barrel in his mouth, and would have ended the shell of what had once been Ray Haus except that the other men stopped him.

For the rest of the train ride to the city he sat next to the body of Stuart, who had died, and thought nothing, said nothing, and for the following thirty-five years he has thought or said nothing and now lives in a care home where he sits, day after day. They feed him and sometimes he watches television but doesn't say anything and apparently does not hear anything and gives no indication of life except that at intervals, usually while he is eating, he will begin to cry and the tears will run down his bearded cheeks into the corners of his mouth to mix with the food as he chews and swallows automatically, like a machine.

16

☐ Somewhere in Minnesota

Alan didn't come by to talk to her and he didn't call and when it was nine o'clock and she realized he wasn't coming Sue became furious. At least he could call, she thought, he could call. But in a few minutes the anger burned off and she began to think of Alan as he really was, what she really knew about him—which was nothing.

She had seen him once drunk and he had come by and taken her to lunch and that was it. He had said nothing about himself, other than that he was from the Leech Lake area. She did not know where he was from, what he had been doing, how old he was—nothing. Anger gave way to reason and she thought she had been silly and in the end was glad that he had not come by, had not called. That was the end of it and that was probably for the best. Tomorrow was coming and she would call Bob and talk to him and get that going again, if indeed it had stopped. He was nice and had that nice smile and it would work out for the best.

It had been a long time since she spent an evening quietly at home with her mother and grandfather. She sat with them and talked, or mostly listened, and had a very enjoyable time. Well, almost enjoyable. They sat in the small kitchen and drank tea, which her grandfather sweetened until it was nearly thick with sugar, and the two older people talked of their childhoods and she listened and learned.

Some of it good. Some of it not so good. Her grandfather had been raised in the woods, in a lodge, and was old enough to remember that it all wasn't wonderful. They had famine in the winters and as a young boy he saw other children starve until their resistance had been lowered and they would die from a cold or minor illness. He spoke differently of his real life, did not tell of it in the high-pitched song he used to tell the stories, and she found herself listening differently. When his tea ran out she would refill it and sometimes interrupt to ask questions, and her mother would cut in with additions when she could remember a detail. And when it was finally eleven and they cleaned the kitchen to go to bed Sue had never felt so close to either her mother or her grandfather.

They were a family. That's what hit her as she was wiping the dishes. We're a family. She stopped wiping and watched her mother empty the washbasin in the sink, saw that her hair bun had come loose and a strand of gray-black thick hair hung down her back. Her mother had glorious hair, thick and rich even at her age, and Sue had the same hair and sometimes when she combed her own she felt as if she were somehow combing her mother's hair.

"What is the matter?" Her mother stopped rinsing the sink with the hose sprayer. "Why are you looking at me that way?"

"I was just thinking that we are very lucky."

Her mother nodded. "Now we are. We weren't always. But now we have all the luck we need." She smiled. "Why is it that you are home this evening? Wasn't there a date or anything?"

Sue laughed. "I was stood up."

"By Bob?"

"No. A new man I met. He took me to lunch yesterday and we had a date tonight."

"You must be losing your touch."

They both laughed and turned out the lights and went upstairs to bed where her grandfather had already gone, pulling himself up the steps carefully and slowly. Sue slid between the sheets with the strange feeling that she was somehow a little girl again. She fell into sleep smiling and slept deeply, without moving, until five o'clock in the morning.

There was first light, false dawn, and she was awakened by a persistent, gentle tapping. When she opened her eyes in the gray light through the window she did not know immediately why she was awake. Usually she slept in on weekends, usually because she went out Friday night. But waking up at dawn was insane and she rolled over and started back to sleep.

Again the knocking, this time a bit louder. She opened her eyes. There was an elm in the back and the wind might be pushing a limb against the window—it was that gentle, rhythmic, spaced tapping—and she went to the window to break the limb off.

It was Alan.

He was standing in the backyard, holding up a broken-off piece of willow with the leaves left on the end, tapping her window. When he saw her at the window he lowered the branch and smiled and motioned for her to open the window.

She momentarily toyed with the idea of just turning away, but realized that he would probably stay out there and keep tapping the window and keep her awake. She slid the window up, or tried to. It was an old house and the windows had been painted many times and the paint jammed and she could only get it open seven or eight inches so she had to get down on her knees and speak through the small opening.

"Go away!"

"I cannot." He put the branch down and stood with his hands to his sides, looking up at the window. "I cannot."

"What do you mean, you can't? Of course you can. Now go away." She tried to slam the window down dramatically but the paint had pinched and jammed and it wouldn't budge. Instead she turned away and moved to the side of the window and stood with her arms crossed. There was no further tapping and she resisted looking out the window and was about to go back to her bed when she heard the window next to hers being pulled open and her grandfather's voice echoed in the backyard.

"Who are you out there?"

"I am Alan, Grandfather. I have come for your granddaughter."

Oh, she thought. Now her grandfather was involved. Next her mother would be opening her window and they could have a conversation and maybe a picnic and . . . she went back to the window. "I'll be right down. Go around to the front."

"Tell me, Alan," her grandfather called. "I am curious. Why do you want my granddaughter?"

"I think it is a thing that is supposed to be."

"I think she is too skinny. She is not round."

"Maybe she can be made fat."

"I don't know. I don't think so. She does not eat enough fat. She cuts the fat off the side of the meat and won't eat it. Somebody like that will never get round. No matter what I tell her she cuts the meat away from the fat."

That was as much as Sue wanted to hear and she ran down the stairs and opened the front door. "I'm around here," she called, standing with a bathrobe wrapped about her body. Her skinny body, she thought. "I'm in front."

"Your grandfather," Alan said, coming around

the corner of the house, "is a nice old man. A nice old man to listen to."

"Do you have any idea what time it is?"

"Yes. It is morning."

"Aren't you just a little late?" She could feel her anger rising, though tempered by curiosity. "I mean for last night? Or am I wrong? Weren't you supposed to come by last night?"

"Something happened. I could not come."

"And you couldn't call?"

He looked at her for a moment, standing in front of her evenly, his hands not moving, his eyes appraising her face. "You are angry."

"Well," she said. "You're not stupid. Yes. I'm angry. Wouldn't you be?"

Again the even gaze, the quiet eyes. "I do not know. Yes, I think I would be. Why don't you get dressed and we will go."

"Go? Are you crazy? Go where? It's five in the morning!"

"Yes. It's morning, I know that. If you get dressed we can go. I will wait out here if you like."

She slammed the door. He was so frustrating! Come at five in the morning and expect her to get dressed and go off with him and not even call when he didn't show up for a date and no excuse

. . . but she did not go back upstairs immediately. She stood inside the door for a time, her back to the wall. Again the anger burned away rapidly and her hand found the knob without really meaning it and she opened the door.

He was still standing there, straight and even.

She said, "Come in. I will make coffee and you can have a cup while I get dressed." She wanted to feel anger, or frustration, but it didn't come. Instead there was the intense interest she had before, the curiosity, and the strange warm feeling she couldn't understand but liked. She put the electric pot on and went upstairs where she put on jeans and a T-shirt. It took her a couple of minutes to comb her hair out and fix her eyes and then she went back downstairs. He was still sitting at the kitchen table, his hands in front of him.

"That did not take long," he said, standing when she came into the kitchen. "Are you ready to go?"

"Shouldn't we have some coffee?"

"I do not drink coffee. But if you would like some you could bring a Thermos."

"Where are we going?"

"There is something I wish to show you and we will probably be gone all day. Perhaps longer."

"You seem awfully sure that I will go."

"If you weren't going to go you wouldn't have let me in." This time a small smile flicked across his face, an up-and-down motion. "I am glad that you did. Shall we go now? I would like for you to see something."

She poured coffee in a Thermos and screwed the lid and cup down and turned. "I'm ready."

"Perhaps we should take your car. You would not like to walk seven miles yet."

"Or ever." She got her car keys and they went outside and got in the car and when the engine was running she turned to him. "Which way?"

"Head out of town north. I'll tell you when to turn off."

She backed out the driveway and started north out Main Street, which became Highway 1 north. The car rode smoothly and she concentrated on the feeling of it—just enjoying the driving—until they were a mile or so north of town. Then she turned to him again.

"Where are we going?"

"To my home. At first. Then to another place I wish to show you."

It was all he would say and she decided to stop pushing. Her anger was completely gone now and she was enjoying the morning. With the window down she could hear birdsongs in the soft morning wind as she passed the green trees. She had almost forgotten he was sitting next to her.

"Here," he said suddenly. "Slow down here and turn in at the next road across the ditch."

She slowed and saw the pull-off—it wasn't a road at all—and pulled into it. There it ended, twenty feet off the highway, and she stopped the car. A footpath led into the thick green forest. He opened the door and got out. "You may wish to bring the Thermos."

She got out, put the Thermos on the ground, and locked the car and he started down the path and she followed, grateful that she had worn tennis shoes and jeans and hadn't tried to be dressier. She was immediately assailed by a swarm of mosquitos, a cloud so dense that she had to breathe through her nostrils and they hit any exposed skin like a fuzzy gray blanket. In seconds she was feeling the sting as they dipped in and she slapped at them ineffectually. When she hit one, a thousand more came, and then still more until she was walking in a cloud of them, weaving down the trail behind Alan. When, finally, they came to the edge of a small lake into a clearing she could see that they did not bother Alan. She was sweaty and bug-bitten and getting mad again.

"They're tearing me apart!" She brushed them away again, but they came back. Her face felt all welts. "Why don't they bother you?"

"Because of what I eat. I am sorry. Wait a moment and I'll fix it for you."

He took a strip of birchbark from a tree, a tiny strip, and some dead small twigs and made a small fire. On this he put eight or ten poplar leaves, green leaves, and they immediately gave off a thick, blue-gray smoke.

"Stand over the fire," he said. "Let the smoke come up in your clothes and hair. Quickly now, while it is thick."

She started to argue. Nothing worked like repellent and she had forgotten her can of spray. But the mosquitos were joined now by deer flies and small black flies and horse flies and it was all too much. She stood, straddling the fire, and squinted the smoke away and coughed and held her breath.

And it worked.

The fire went out almost at once and the smoke drifted away but the bugs didn't come back. "That's incredible. Just incredible."

"It is what they did when the food was not good enough. If they could not always control the insects with the odor they gave off from the food they could make smoke. It will last most of the day. The insects do not like the smoke."

He was so formal. "Insects" rather than "bugs." And now when he talked his hands moved and flowed—up like birds they moved. And somehow the smoke seemed to make the itching go away. "Is this where you live?" It was just an open clearing next to the lake, a circle of still, flat-mirror water. "Where do you sleep?"

"On the ground. Sometimes out there." He pointed out on the lake.

"On the water? How do you do that?"

"In my canoe. Come, follow me again." He left the clearing and went to the edge of the water, then turned and walked a short way down the shoreline. She followed—the bugs still ignored her—and watched as he pulled a canoe out of some willows.

It was a birchbark canoe, made in the old tradition, with heated pitch covering the seams that had been laced with strips of bark. All of ash and willow, with graceful ribs, the white-yellow bark had such a delicate quality that it almost looked like crocheting.

"It's beautiful," she said, catching her breath. "Truly beautiful. Where did you get it?"

"I made it. There was an old man—a white man—up north of here who makes them the old way and I lived with him and helped him and he showed me the way." He removed two hand-carved ash paddles from the bottom of the canoe and gently slid the graceful shape onto the water where it floated as light as thistle-down. "Get in. We have miles to go. Bring the Thermos if you like. And watch so your feet stay on the willow floor grate or they will poke through the bark."

Sue nodded. She had fished in canoes when she was young, fished with her grandfather on several occasions and went wild ricing with him once—always in aluminum canoes. But she knew how to get in, putting her weight on the sides with her hands, and she carefully worked her way to the bow where she knelt and held a hand back for the paddle. Alan handed it to her and she steadied the canoe by sticking the paddle down into the mud while he got in and settled on his knees. Then he stroked and she matched his pull and the canoe shot out across the early-morning still water. She looked down next to them in the water and saw her reflection slide on the water, broken by the ripples from the bow when her paddle moved forward, then again when she pulled.

Silence.

The silence was alive for seconds, then cut by birdsongs, then silence again, and through it all, above it all, came the keening song of a loon out ahead of them on the lake, a song that belonged with the canoe and Alan and belonged with her soul and she turned to say something but he was sitting with his face down and his eyes closed, letting the canoe coast, and she turned back to the front without making a sound. It was better to not talk. And everything rolled into a ball for her, a round ball in her mind made up of working at the bank and her grandfather still being alive and his song-stories and her mother's loose hair hanging down the night before and the beauty of the bark canoe and the strength that was Alan that came from the rear of the canoe and moved up through the sides and was the canoe and was Alan and was the water and was her.

Is me.

And she wondered if she had fallen in love.

And she wondered if she had really learned something about herself or only thought she had; wondered if the artist came again and did her portrait she would say she was Indian and not Samoan or whatever it was; wondered if she would ever be the same again as before the bark canoe and Alan and the smooth lake and the high-cry, the wild high-cry of the loon and this time when she turned she saw him sitting straight and even, the paddle dripping drops of silver into the still water, his eyes on her, evenly, knowing, all-knowing, and she knew she would not be the same again.

Ever.

And she was glad.

She reached forward with the paddle again, pulled the water back to her, felt Alan's paddle match hers, felt the canoe take force, take purpose, and knew that she would not be the same again and that from now on she would never be what she was again and was glad.

Tonight, this night, she would bring Alan to her grandfather. They would eat and they would listen to the story he told and she would share this with him, share it with Alan.

Her grandfather was still alive.

17

☐ Somewhere in Nebraska

At the middle time of the day when the sun was beating straight down on his back, David heard a horn sound but did not look up or stop hoeing until he saw the others drop their hoes where they were and walk back down the field. Then he dropped his hoe and he could not straighten, could not rise without difficulty and his hands were cramped in the shape of the hoe handle. He tried to stretch, felt all the muscles in his back and neck tear at themselves, felt the burn on his neck from the sun, felt every part of his body that seemed to hurt, but he started walking with the rest toward where the farmer waited with the truck.

In the back of the pickup were a cardboard box full of sandwiches and a large cooler full of cold water. David started to grab several sandwiches but saw a disapproving look from the pregnant woman and he put two of them back. Chihuahua dies hard, he thought—in Chihuahua if you did not grab, somebody would take the whole box and you would have nothing.

They ate in silence, sitting along the fence. David was starved and the sandwiches were of peanut butter and jelly and the sweetness of the jelly tasted wonderful to him. He drank cold water between sandwiches, and ate four of them, and was still not full. But he noticed that the others would not eat more than two. He was sitting next to the pregnant woman and when he was done eating he leaned back against a rock, happy for the rest. "Tell me," he said, "is it this way always?"

She did not at first answer and he thought she was not going to. But after shifting her stomach she answered him in Spanish. "I am not sure what you mean. Is what like this always?"

"Do they always feed you in this manner? And bring you water in this manner? I did not hear them talk of this in the cantina in Chi—at my home."

Again she moved and this time she did not answer but looked across the road at another sugar-beet field on the other side, or so he thought, though she could have been just looking at the sky. It was as if he were not there. To her far side the old man he had at first spoken to laughed. "No. It is not always like this. It is never like this. It is not what you think it is now and it will never be what you think it is."

"I do not understand."

"No. You most certainly do not. You are from Chihuahua, are you not?"

David debated lying, decided it would be futile. "Yes. I have been here only three, no, four days and already I have found work. It is not to be believed." He could not keep a smugness out of his voice, the hard edge of pride. "I have been very lucky...."

"I have been very lucky." The pregnant woman snorted and mimicked him. "Listen to the little cockroach talk of his luck. Lucky. Listen, lucky person, if you are hoeing beets you are not lucky. Lucky people do not hoe beets. Lucky people own the farms that hire us to hoe the beets. Lucky people sell the beets to the sugar plants to make the sugar. Lucky people sell the sugar and get the money. Lucky people do not hoe beets."

David was silent for a time, surprised by the outburst. Then he shrugged. "All this is true, I suppose. But still, is not twenty-one dollars an acre a good amount of money?"

This time she did not scorn him but rather looked on him with pity, a softening in her eyes, as a mother might see him. "Is that what you think, little one? Did you think you were getting twenty-one dollars for an acre of beets?" She moved again, full of discomfort, and the older man stood and came closer to her, his eyes worried. "Is it all right, Maria? I told you not to work too close to the having of the baby."

"I will be all right. I have had children before, children grown and gone. It will be fine."

"I do not understand," David interrupted. "The man told me he would pay me twenty-one dollars for an acre. Was he lying?"

The others all laughed and the old man laughed but the woman did not and her seriousness made the others become quiet. "How many sandwiches did you eat?"

"I do not know. Three, four perhaps. I do not know."

"You should keep a record of the number,"

Maria said. "And not eat so many. They cost you a dollar for each one."

"What?"

She nodded. "They are a dollar for each one deducted from the amount you have earned this day. The woman who is the farmer's wife sits in the house and makes them and sends them out and for every one you eat they will take a dollar off your money. And the hoe costs another dollar for each day that you use it. A dollar rental. And we must each pay one more dollar for the water he brings to us. A dollar a day for the water. So now, my proud little one, now how much money do you have?"

"But—"

"In this first day you will not hoe more than half an acre. That is ten and a half dollars. If you ate four sandwiches that is four dollars taken away, then another dollar for the water and another dollar for the hoe. You will have worked all this day for four dollars and fifty cents. That is the luck of the beets. Then, tonight, they will give you a plate of *frijoles* with some small amount of pork fat in it and a glass of flavored water and you will have to eat because that is all there is and you must eat. That evening meal costs two dollars and you must wash your own plate afterward.

Then, tomorrow morning, you will be given some more of those same *frijoles* and that will be another dollar and fifty cents before you start the day. So when tomorrow is done there will be that much more to deduct. You have worked this day for two dollars and fifty cents. Tomorrow will be only slightly better." Now Maria smiled at him, but it was a kind smile. "That is the luck of the beets. That is how lucky you are, little one. You have so much luck that you are hoeing beets."

"Surely you are mistaken. If it is so bad we can go somewhere else to work. There are many beets, are there not?"

"It is always the same." The old man stood and Maria got to her feet, only much slower now. "They are all the same. It is the way of how this works, the method of this business of the luck of the beets. There is not another way for it to be."

"But it is not fair."

"No." Maria reached out and ruffled his hair. "No, it is not fair. Now you are beginning to see how it is with the beets. But it is something we can do and down there we can do nothing. That is the way it works. That is what you call the luck, the luck of the beets. And now, now we must go back to work."

They all stood and went to where they had left

their hoes at different places in the field. David followed them and leaned down and picked up his hoe and his back was stiff and his legs were stiff and his hands were cramped and the blisters were broken and bleeding and were resealing into calluses and he let the hoe swing out, almost by itself, and cut a beet, then another beet, and again, and again, the hoe pulling him down the field, beet to beet, and he kept thinking that this day of his life he would make only two dollars and fifty cents.

What a thing that is, he thought, to spend a day of one's life for two dollars and fifty cents. He tried to shrug and to think that in Chihuahua he would spend a day and more than a day and a week and more than a week and not get two dollars and fifty cents but that somehow did not make it better.

He could not make it work in his mind that one day of one's life was worth only two dollars and fifty cents. He was not angry yet and perhaps he would not get angry but he was uncomfortable with the feeling and the hoe would hit harder on the beet tops, harder and harder with the discomfort of the feeling that a day of one's life should be worth more than two dollars and fifty cents.

And so that day passed, passed into and through the heat of the afternoon when his mouth was as dry as the sand in Chihuahua's desert, into the muggy heat of the day. Passed through beets and more beets until it was nearly dark and he heard the horn—it made him angry now—and he dropped his hoe and stood, slowly, letting the creaks in his back work out, stood and walked with the rest back to the truck.

They climbed in the rear of the pickup and rode to the farm and were fed at an outside table on metal plates from a big pot of pinto beans the woman at the farm brought out. In the pot was a single large piece of pork belly and there was day-old bread to soak up the juice and he thought it tasted all right, as well as the sugared water, but when he thought that it was costing him two dollars of his day of life he did not think it was so good. Again, there was not anger yet, but the discomfort was there and he ate and ate until his stomach was tight and still did not think it was worth the two dollars of a day of his life.

After they had finished eating—there were plenty of beans and bread—the others stood and went to some small huts in back of the round metal granaries near the curved-roof barn. But the farmer told David he would have to sleep in the feed room of the barn and David followed him where he led. In the back there was a small room and he went into it and fashioned a bed from the feed sacks. It was dusty and sneezy but it was dry and he was so tired that he did not care. He closed his eyes and was asleep and gone without thinking and did not move, did not twitch, until seven hours later when the farmer opened the door to the feed room and awakened him.

"Up. Come on, it will be light soon and the beets are waiting."

He followed the farmer out into the predawn gray light and the others were up and already at the table and he sat there and the pot of beans came from the house again. The same pot with added beans but the same piece of fat and some flat-black coffee so strong and vicious that David could not drink it.

They ate rapidly, spooning down the beans to get it done, and were into the truck again and back out to the field where the hoes lay waiting where they had been dropped the night before. The hoes lay waiting.

And the beets.

They went back to work in silence, went to their different places in the field, and David began chopping, swinging the hoe now in a rhythm, working down the rows and not seeing the sun come up, not seeing the morning truly start, not hearing the songs of the meadowlarks. Just the beets. Only the beets that would take this day of his life until it was dark again and there would be the beans again and the same piece of fat again and the beets would take another day, another day of his life, and the discomfort began to grow and he would have been angry then, would have allowed the anger to take him except that he heard cries from ahead in the field and he looked up to see that Maria was down, had dropped her hoe and was down on her back and everybody was running to her.

For a second David hesitated—they were, after all, not his people. But in a way they were his people, they were all of the beets, all the people with the hoes, so he threw his hoe to the ground and ran to Maria as well. Not thinking what he could do, but running.

When he arrived he could tell that it was her time, that the baby was coming, and he stooped over her while the old man knelt beside her to help and she was pushing and David turned away at first because this was not a thing for him to watch. But he didn't turn all the way away because he had never seen this thing and the others had not turned away but moved to give her shade with their bodies from the morning sun and he did the same and decided that while he could not actually watch it all it would be proper or at least allowable to watch parts of it. He saw her heels, bare now because she had kicked off her rubber slaps, saw her heels dig into the black earth and push when she contracted and heard her short sharp cries when the pains came, saw the heels and heard the cries. He felt that the earth had become one with the cries and the pain, that the earth came up through her heels when they dug into the dirt and then the cries came closer and the heels dug deeper and pushed and pushed into the beets and he saw the baby come, new and shiny, and felt that at that moment it was all right to look and he did and the old man lifted the baby with great tenderness and wiped its mouth clean and put it on Maria's stomach, all in the new sun of the morning in the fresh dirt of the field with the baby making small sounds, not crying but small sounds, and David thought of the beauty of it. It was a moment when he thought of the beauty of it and knew that he would remember it for the rest of however many days he had and he looked for the first time up to her face and in that moment, for that split second in time, he saw that she had become something close to the Madonna, saw that she was lifted above the field and above the pain and then her face changed, contracted in a grimace, and she screamed and started digging with her heels again, holding her hands over the face of the baby and sliding on her back in the dirt and David thought she was afraid of them, all of them standing around her.

"We must move," he said aloud. "We are bothering her. She is trying to hide the baby from us. See. See how she moves?"

But the old man shook his head and put his hand on her head and soothed her and made small sounds to quiet her and leaned down and she whispered something into his ear and he nodded and took his hat off and covered the baby's head with it, covered the whole baby with the hat, and he turned up to them and David could see the white line where the hat had stopped the sun on his forehead and the old man made a small smile, a smile of apology. "It is the beets. She wishes to hide the baby from the beets."

Ahh, David thought, of course. She does not like the beets and she wished to hide the baby from the beets and he thought then it was such a savage thing, that she should hate the beets so much and fear the beets so much, such a savage thing.

Then he turned and walked slowly back to where his hoe lay in the dirt between the rows of beets and he picked it up and began to cut them, cut them with the sharp edge of steel and felt the anger come. The slow anger. And he wondered if the anger would last him the rest of his life.

18

☐ Somewhere in Montana

Laura went through the kitchen without stopping for food. But halfway up the stairs she realized how hungry she was and though it was now eleven-thirty and she was tired beyond belief, she went to the refrigerator and took out some bread and slices of lunch meat and made two bare sandwiches. She ate one standing by the refrigerator door, almost without tasting it, then took out the milk and poured herself a glass and took it and the second sandwich to her room. There she turned on the light and sat on the edge of the bed, chewing and drinking the milk, letting her eyes run over the walls.

Posters and pictures of horses. Ribbons she'd won for riding and for raising good sheep, fair ribbons and Four-H ribbons and one rodeo ribbon she'd taken for barrel racing when she was still really young and before she started to truly work the ranch and understand ranching. As she thought she did now. Her whole life was on the walls. A picture standing next to a pickup with a blond boy named Henson—Hen. A time that had passed. Her whole life on the walls.

Her eyes burned with lack of sleep and she lay back on the bed and closed them, but sleep wouldn't come. She didn't set the alarm or take off her clothes, except to kick her boots off, and the barn smell hung around her. She did not know how long she would have lain that way, in the smell and with her anger still primed, except that she heard her father's measured stride below in the kitchen and then coming up the stairs.

She reached over and turned out the light and pulled the coverlet over her body and faked sleep, but he knew better and opened the door and came in and sat on the edge of her bed.

"You're some punkins, you are." It was something he'd always said to her when she was small. Called her "some punkins." Now it made her cry, his sitting there in the semidarkness. "I found you a doughnut. You want it?"

"Well . . ." She turned over and pulled the light cord, sat up. "It's probably stale anyway—fits my mood." She took the doughnut and it was stale, but she took a bite and chewed.

"You still mad?"

She nodded, chewing. "Some. It wasn't right, what I said. But I'm still some mad."

He rubbed his face with dirty hands, tried to rub the exhaustion away, but it stayed. "The lambs look good. Maybe the best yet."

She started to say something acid about not being part of it any longer but sensed that he wanted to say more and decided to hold back. "It's those Columbia-cross ewes. They're tough and throw strong—throw real strong."

He nodded. "Yes. And Louie, and you, and your mama. We all add up to making one hell of a team."

It surprised her because he never had used strong language before and she could see now that he was very serious and wanted to talk and she sat up in the bed and leaned back against the headboard. "Yes. We do."

Again he nodded, but he wasn't listening to her now. "I've never been part of that before, that kind of thing. Always I've been alone until I met your mama, and then Louie came along and then you. But before that I was alone. I came back from the service and I saw this land and I had money I'd saved and I came up with it but there was nobody to help me. Nobody. My family, they were a joke—a bad joke. My daddy, he was so bad in drink that he died of his liver when I was a young boy, and my mama, she ran off with the man who came to deliver fuel oil, and there wasn't anybody else. I got put with an uncle who was dirt mean and when I got old enough to leave, I left. With just my clothes and a broke-down old plug horse named Willy I took and left and that uncle, he tried to get me for stealing the horse. Liked to work me to death and never gave me a dime and then tried to get me for stealing the horse. Ha. Horse died before I'd gone twenty miles and I hitchhiked and lied my way into getting hired over in Wyoming."

He paused and she wanted to reach out a hand to him, started to move her hand, but held back. He had never told her anything of his childhood before, never said anything about his youth at all. She had a picture of him taken just before the army, on her dresser, and she looked up at it now and tried to see him as a young boy.

"But I said then that I would get me some money and I would get me some land and I would never be owing to anybody. I would get me some land and some cows—later I went for sheep, but at first it was cows. I would get me some land and cows and I would make a place I could live on and it would be my place, all my place, and it would be a good place."

Another pause. He took a breath and this time she touched his shoulder and there were tears sliding down her cheeks. "You did it."

"And I did it." Still he did not hear her. "I worked alone and I built a wooden barn and slept upstairs in the loft and then a work shed and finally a house and every nail, every board I did myself. And I kept saying, kept saying that someday I would make it work and I would have a place and it would be my place. I kept saying that. And after some years of scrabbling, scrabbling more than we do now, and eating pinto beans and tough meat, one morning I came out of the house—only had one big room then—and there were some cows and a couple of horses and I didn't owe nobody, *nobody*. And you know what I felt? You know?"

She shook her head.

"I felt so damn lonely I thought I would die,

that's what I felt. So along came your mama and I knew that I couldn't have a place alone and we got married and then Louie came, just riding in one day, and he stayed and then you came. Slick as a calf. And I'll tell you true, I kind of had my head set on a boy then. But not now. Not ever now. I tell you, punkins, I don't think there is any way I could have got luckier and done better than you—that's a natural fact."

She glowed. "I was wrong to talk that way—I was just tired. You know. Lambing and all."

Now he shook his head. "No. You were right. You're almost always right, except when you were small. I thought I was doing the right thing because I thought you were missing some of those things you ought to get. You haven't got a steady boy—"

"I date," she said. "I've had several—I haven't met one yet that I thought would last. I will, though."

"I know that, I know that. But see, I thought keeping you working like we did was wrong and was keeping you from that. But your mama and me, we talked it over and she said I was wrong. That you are part of this, part of all that I started as much as I am, and it would be wrong to push you away even if I thought it was right, even if I thought it was for your own good." He sighed and stood. "And I don't want what I had. When I was alone and walked out that morning and saw the cows and horses and was lonely—I don't want that ever again. That was some kind of empty feeling, that was."

Laura smiled. "You won't have it. Not while I'm alive, you won't be lonely."

"Well, just you keep me from kicking the bucket over now and again and we'll do just fine. Now you'd best get back out to the barn. The lambs keep coming—just keep coming."

"I'll be along." He left and for a time she sat on the bed, looking at the walls, the posters, crying alone, thinking how lucky she was, how incredibly lucky to have gotten a father like him. Then she stood and wiped her eyes and turned out the light and headed for the barn.

The lambs kept coming.

19

☐ Somewhere in Colorado

Peter came onto the stage in Red Rocks and let the sound from the audience swell around him, hold him, carry him. For a time, a delicate time that he held as long as he could, he did not speak, did not touch his guitar, which hung around his neck, but stood and held his arms out to the sides in gratitude and let the sound hold him. It was like a friend holding him, the moment he cared for most in concerts, when they welcomed him.

Then he turned and pointed to the band, winked at Mike who stood smiling over the keyboard because he knew, he knew. The rest of the band had knowledge of music, and knew that what they had with Peter's new sound was good. But Mike was inside of Peter, knew Peter, knew what they had was better than good.

When the peak of the welcome had subsided to an even roar he went to the microphone and held up his hands for silence.

"You are wonderful!" His voice boomed and they screamed to match it. "You are wonderful and I am glad to be here and there can be nothing better than this—nothing better than us, you, the band, me. Thank you. Thank you for being here."

More roaring. When it went down again he lowered his voice, almost whispered into the microphone now, brought them closer to him. "We have something for you, something just for you. We have a new sound."

More swelling of noise, welling, up past him into the huge red rocks that gave the foothills outdoor auditorium its name, the thunder of the crowd reverberating until the band was swamped in it.

Peter turned his back to them, looked at the band, saw that they were waiting, ready, and he took the first note, took it out of his head and put it into the guitar.

Rising.

It was the clear rising note that led to the falling

note that brought them all together and the band came in on the edges of it, made it grow into something alive, more than music, a heartbeat, a pulse of beautiful rising sound that quieted the audience, stopped them.

For the first part Peter did not sing—although in rehearsals he came in with the song almost at once. But performing was a living thing, each performance different, almost with a distinct soul of its own, and he was with them now, with the audience, with the band, with the rocks, and he let the sound work alone for a time, rising, filling, going out into the crowd and mixing with them and coming back and going out again until there was not a difference among any of them, the crowd, the band, the music. All had mixed, all were one.

Rising.

And when the time was right, perfectly right, and the sound of the music had made the gates open he moved up to the microphone, closed his eyes, and brought in the words.

> *"We've been down,*
> *the same road, the same road.*
> *Why didn't we go together?"*

He sang it low, with a throaty voice, way below the music but coming along with it, as if his voice and the music were on the same road and would be coming together and at the end of the simple verse, the clean verse, the music fell off a bit and he brought up his voice a bit and they met and he backed away from the microphone, turned from it, let the music come back up and took some side chords on his guitar, let Mike fill with the keyboard as he turned, then, back to the microphone.

"We're going down,
the same road, the same road.
Why don't we go together?"

And again he turned away from the microphone, let the music take it and felt the flow go from the words into the music, felt the song go out and mix with the crowd and come back stronger, more full.

They all grew. He moved across the stage, moving in time to the music, and leaned down by Mike at the keyboard and Mike felt it and smiled and mouthed, "Incredible," with his lips and kept playing and Peter floated. Floating now, he went

159

back to the microphone and repeated the last verse.

> *"We're going down,*
> *the same road, the same road.*
> *Why don't we go together?"*

And then he sang it again, and again, and yet again, letting the verse grow and build with the music and the music pulse with the words until they were all the same, the band, the crowd, Peter, the words, all the same and on cue, with a drop of his hand, he stopped it. Stopped it all. The music, the sound, the singing, the band all stopped at once, instantly, and the silence was so intense, so wildly intense and sudden and new, that there was not a movement, not a sound.

No, Peter thought. I've done this wrong. They didn't like it. They're not clapping and they didn't understand or feel what I understood and felt and they're not part of the music. He turned and held his hand out to Mike and felt a great sadness because he thought he had lost the people, the audience who had to be part of the music for it to be music at all, and he started to say to Mike that he was sorry, sorry for dragging the band down the wrong way, the wrong way, and the crowd went wild.

It started in the back, a clapping that came to the front, back again, swelling, rolling and growing until they were on their feet, standing and screaming, their arms raised, and they were singing now, singing the last verse over and over, and with a surge they broke through the security guards and flooded onto the stage and a hundred hundred hands lifted Peter and Mike and the rest of the band and moved them with great gentleness up on the top of the hands and passed them up and back and all around the crowd.

Peter found himself singing with them and when they had passed him all around they worked the band back down to the stage and Peter picked up his guitar and hung it around his neck and held up his hands. When there was silence he found the microphone, and he took it from the stand and said, "There is not a line where I end and you begin. We are all one, one thing, one person, one voice. I love you. Thank you." And he meant it then, meant that he loved them. "We are all the same family."

And now they were silent and Peter saw that the band had found their instruments and were ready and he broke into "Hearts," a soft love song from their album, and he sang it for them, for the crowd, and then more songs and still more until the end of the concert. And finally he came up one more time with the new sound and the band grew with the crowd again and then it was done, done, and he and Mike were in Peter's dressing room.

"So," Peter said. "So."

"So." Mike nodded.

Peter studied him. "So where do we go from here?"

"What do you mean?"

"I mean just that. Something happened out there and I don't see how we can go back and just do the same sound over and over the way we used to do. Something happened and we can't just take the money and run, right? It's all different now. So. That's what I mean. So."

Mike smiled. "I'm surprised you can't see it."

"See what?"

"See where we have to go. We have to go back to where the sound came from and we have to find it again, and find the next new sound and keep doing that. Keep doing that."

Peter knew he was right. Suddenly he could see the black lady and the rich blues and he smiled and nodded. "We have to go back to Kansas City and find it again."

"And to all the other Kansas Cities and all the other sounds. We have to do that because that's what we do."

"Yes." Peter nodded. "That's what we do."

"So," Mike said.

"So." Peter grinned. "So let's pack."

20

☰ Battle Hymn Four

When it happens the first thing will be an enormous *CLICK*. Or it might be more of a huge cracking sound—a cross between a crack and a click. It will last only the tiniest part of a second and will be instantaneously followed by a white glare of such intensity that it rivals the sun. . . .

In the high jungles of India there is a protected area for tigers where they can live and hunt without fear of being taken for their pelts, and the cats in the area have come to know this and have lost their nervousness. On the banks of a small river in this preserve, a female Bengal tiger, in full physical prime, is lying on her back nursing her two cubs. The sun is a gold heat shining down to warm her belly and her head is stretched out and she is asleep with the contentment and grace that is unique to nursing mothers. The cubs, greedy, are sucking and kneading with their front paws, forcing more milk out. And because the mother has recently killed, she is full of milk and it comes out a little faster than the cubs can drink and it wets their faces. One cub raises its head and peers intently into the grass at some rustling sound it has heard and a drop of milk begins to slide down a whisker on the left side of its nose, a white jewel in the soft light, and it opens its mouth and begins to stick out the tip of its tongue, steaming with moistness, to catch the droplet of milk on the whisker—just the smallest movement of the pink tip of the curved little tongue on the small cub in the morning new sun *CLICK*.